Dirty Latte

A COFFEE SHOP ROMANCE

SMALL TOWN DIRT
BOOK TWO

REGINA BERGEN

Latte Lovers this way

This book is dedicated to coffee and to anyone who plays a role in the caffeination process: coffee farmers, coffee harvesters, coffee processors, coffee roasters, coffee shop owners, baristas, and—yes—coffee drinkers!

Oh, and also to everyone who believed in me, even when I didn't believe in myself. Without them (and coffee), this book wouldn't exist. I actually don't know for sure if I would exist.

Preface

Latte Lovers this way

Dirty Latte – A Coffee Shop Romance is the second book in the *Small Town Dirt* series, following *Dirty Hoe – A Gardening Romance*. I intentionally wrote these as standalone books that can be read on their own for a full story or in sequence to enjoy the underlying back story as well. Each takes place in the same town with several crossover locations and characters while focusing on a new couple and *their* story.

    Dirty Latte took me by surprise. When I wrote it, I was in a very different place mentally than when I wrote *Dirty Hoe*. At the start of writing, it was planned as a fun, romantic comedy, much like the first. I hadn't expected to dive too deep into anything, really, beyond the love story between the two main characters.

At some point, however, the characters told me to fuck off.

While *Dirty Latte* maintains the contemporary rom-com vibe in many ways, my characters asked me to delve into specific themes, including mental health issues, suicide, and stalking, that I hadn't quite planned to touch on—but also don't regret. The story is primarily light, but certain scenes touch on harsh realities, and I thought it was important to ensure the reader was aware of this before taking it on.

I hope this doesn't sway anyone away from reading—and I did include a content warning for one scene I thought might be particularly problematic for anyone triggered by the theme of suicide—so it won't be a surprise.

With all that said, I genuinely hope you enjoy the book—without darkness, we wouldn't know light.

Welcome to Cold Brew on Main

MORGAN

Chapter 1

MORGAN SLAMMED an empty vat on the counter near the espresso machine, huffing in frustration as she twisted the top off and refilled it with creamer. She typically held her anger in, maintaining a calm external demeanor, especially at work, but the interaction with her last customer had sent her over the edge. *Arrogant, elitist ass,* she thought to herself as she set about cleaning and restocking the coffee preparation area for the next shift, rolling her eyes as she completed each task on autopilot.

Maybe it's me. I've been working a lot of extra hours lately —not that I don't need them, but a good night's sleep sure would be nice. Waking up at the crack of dawn and working until the sun was setting was certainly not sustainable, but the bills didn't stop piling up just because Morgan was tired.

Exhausted, actually. Her only saving grace was that she was employed at a coffee shop, and Ben, the owner, allowed the staff to enjoy as much complimentary caffeination as they wanted—or needed in Morgan's case.

Morgan took a deep breath and counted to ten before releasing it, a technique she'd been working on with her therapist. It was supposed to help her feel calm when she was stressed. She couldn't tell if it helped much, but she figured she might as well try out some of the relaxation exercises that they discussed in their session—at least then she could tell her therapist she was using her "tools." As Morgan was pulling in a second long breath, the bell hanging from the store's front door jingled, signifying someone entering.

"Miss Morgan, my favorite barista!" Ben's good-natured voice came booming across *Cold Brew on Main*.

"Hey, Ben. Correct me if I'm wrong, but aren't I your *only* barista at present?" Morgan tossed Ben a friendly smile. While she wanted to escape from her shift as quickly as possible, Ben and his girlfriend Gia were fabulous bosses, and she was grateful for their kindness. Today, in particular, since Ben had insisted on covering the final shift of the day to give her a break. He even promised to give her the tips generated. Some chitchat was a small price to pay!

"Semantics," Ben said with a chuckle. "You look..." He paused, searching for a word that wouldn't sound too offensive.

"Tired," Morgan finished. "I know. I am. I almost went off on a customer a few minutes ago. He insisted I made the drink wrong. The drink I invented. *My* drink."

"Morgan—"

"I know, I know," Morgan cut him off. "The customer is always right or whatever."

"No. That's not what I was going to say. At all. Sometimes, the customer is flat-out wrong, but you've always been great about making them feel as if they're right—or at least accept that you are—regardless. I was actually going to tell you to go home, get a good night's sleep and take tomorrow off. Gia said she'd be happy to come in to help me tomorrow during the busy parts of the day. I have to roast beans, so I'd be here anyway. We'll have each other's company, and you get a break. You've been spending too much time in this place!"

"My rent is due next week. I appreciate the offer, but I really can't take the day—"

"Shhh," Ben cut her off. "You'll get paid for the day—plus the tips. You've really saved *Cold Brew* since Gia and I have been spending so much time getting the restaurant moving in the right direction. If anyone owes anyone, I owe you!" Ben and Gia had somewhat recently become partners at *Charmed to Table*, a local farm-to-table restaurant, and they were still implementing some changes there.

"Ben, I can't. I—"

"Morgan. Please. I have an interview scheduled this afternoon to get you some backup around here. He seems like a nice guy. You can't be expected to be here for every single shift —and I can't always fill in to give you the time off you deserve. We'll get this place back to normal soon enough with a new team."

"You know I am grateful, Ben, but the truth is that I need those shifts, anyway. You know that."

"How about a raise? Promotion to manager should make a few days off during the week possible, right? It certainly wasn't easy to lose both of our other baristas at once, but I guess you can't control other people's elopements," Ben said with a chuckle. "And who could begrudge them the right to travel the world together?" He winked at Morgan, knowing she was well aware of his globe-trekking past life as an eco-tourism mogul.

Morgan's jaw dropped. "Seriously? A manager? Me?"

"Absolutely. Well-deserved. You've been handling this place on your own for weeks—or has it been months? I don't even know anymore. Let's see how this interview goes. If not this guy, someone else will come through soon enough. We'll get you the break you need with pay that keeps you in your apartment. You've proven yourself an irreplaceable asset to *Cold Brew,* and we'll do whatever we must to keep you!"

Morgan threw her arms around Ben and gave him a friendly hug. "Thank you. I honestly can't thank you and Gia enough. You've been so amazing. You've honestly saved me after—" Morgan paused for a moment, searching for the right words. "After... everything. When my ex left, I would have lost my apartment without all those extra hours—and if I were you, I would have fired me back then. I certainly wasn't performing at my best."

Ben waved his hand dismissively. "Aww, shucks," he said. "Well, Gia and I already talked this over, and we're all on the same page—we just need to fill some of these shifts. Now, get out of here! Go relax or sleep or party or... something!"

"Yes, Boss." Morgan pushed herself onto her tiptoes, using the counter to lengthen the stretch. She'd been on her feet for hours, like usual, but this time, her body was feeling it. She couldn't wait to return to her apartment, lie down, close her eyes, and crash. She hoped she'd sleep well into the next day!

With a quick wave, Morgan grabbed her bag and walked out the front door and toward the bus stop on Main Street. Unfortunately, even with all the extra hours, owning a car wasn't within her budget. So, public transportation, it was! She didn't mind, though. Morgan enjoyed sitting back and letting someone else drive her home after a long day of fueling customers with caffeine and calories. It felt a little strange heading home in the daylight, though. Lately, most of her transportation occurred in the early morning or evening hours, and the opportunity to read her book on the bus in the light of the sun felt like a rare gift.

As the bus pulled up to the curb by the stop and Morgan glanced back toward *Cold Brew*, her eyes narrowed. The same customer who had given her a hard time about his drink was turning the corner, walking directly toward the café! *What's he doing going back inside? Did he see me leave? I hope that pompous ass isn't going in there to complain about me to Ben. I can't afford to lose that manager role before I even have it!*

As she watched him walk up the stairs and enter *Cold Brew*, she couldn't stop herself from thinking: *It'd be a whole lot easier to dislike him if he wasn't so damn handsome...*

The Test

JET

Chapter 2

JET MUMBLED under his breath as he walked back toward *Cold Brew on Main.* He had been there only an hour ago to check it out and get a sense of the coffee shop's vibe and atmosphere. It was a cool place with a casual, fun, artsy vibe. The coffee was roasted and ground on-site, coming from sustainable fair-trade harvests worldwide. But... *What a bitch,* he thought, re-playing his interaction with the café's barista again in his mind. *A pretty bitch, all the same.*

Jet was an experienced barista, having worked at a commercial coffee chain for several years before moving to be closer to the rest of his bandmates, who were sharing a loft apartment in the small downtown area. All he did was point out that the ratio of foam to beverage seemed off based on the drink's menu description, and the barista looked like she was going to take his head off. Jet rolled his eyes. He was only trying to help.

As he approached *Cold Brew* again, he spotted the same barista slipping out the front of the building and walking in his direction. Not wanting to revisit their discussion about coffee-to-foam ratios, he ducked into a narrow alleyway between two buildings until she passed. He glanced over his shoulder just as she reached the bus stop, pulled a book out from her bag, and sat on a bench to read. *I mean, she reads. That's a plus,* Jet thought. *Maybe she was having an off day. She did look tired.*

He shrugged and continued toward *Cold Brew* to meet with Ben, the owner, for his job interview. The online ad indicated they were looking for a barista, but Jet hoped they might also be looking for a store manager—or that an opportunity might arise once he got his foot in the door.

Jet arrived with a few minutes to spare but figured there was no harm in being early. Pulling the door open, he stepped into *Cold Brew* for the second time that day, grateful that the barista from earlier had left. Standing behind the counter now was a well-put-together but casually dressed man. Jet strode over and waited behind the only person in line, figuring he might as well grab another drink should he have to wait around a bit to meet with Ben.

As the lady in front of him took her beverage from the man behind the counter, Jet stepped forward.

"Hey there, what can I get for you?" Ben asked with a friendly smile. He had always been great with customers, and his welcoming demeanor was part of his success in his many business ventures. Clients loved working *with* Ben, and employees loved working *for* him. He was laid back and made it easy for everyone to get on the same page, even amid complicated, sometimes delicate, business decisions.

"Hello. I'm here to meet with the owner. Ben, I believe. I have an appointment."

"Ahh, you must be Jethro! Nice to meet you," Ben said, causing Jet to wince at the sound of his full name. "You're looking at him. It's pretty slow right now, and my girlfriend Gia is in the back, bagging some coffee for retail. She can take over up here for a bit. Let's talk. Want a drink?"

"Yes, that'd be great. Thank you. Oh, and it's Jet, by the way. I go by Jet," he said, flashing a grin at Ben.

"Jet. I like it. Jet it is. If you want a drink, then get back here and make it. Make two. Three, actually. I'm sure Gia's ready for more caffeine! Barista's choice. Consider it an informal test." Ben chuckled.

Jet's eyes lit up. If there was one thing he could do, it was prepare a solid coffee drink. Jet strode confidently behind the counter without a second thought and began assessing the barista station to see what he was working with. It seemed like a pretty standard setup—a commercial espresso machine with milk-frothing pitchers, steam wands, tamping mats, various flavored syrups, and so on. *I can work with this,* thought Jet, grabbing three cups from a stack nearby.

"You like chocolate?" asked Jet

"Who doesn't?"

"Does your wife?" Jet gestured to the third cup.

"Girlfriend," Ben corrected, then winked. "For now, anyway. And yes, she does. Thank you."

"Alrighty." Jet flipped a cup in the air, catching it with the other hand. "Let's do this!"

Ben grinned at Jet. "I like your enthusiasm," he said as Jet began to pour espresso shots and steam the milk for the drinks.

"Wait till you taste my drinks," Jet said, a smile dancing up the corners of his mouth. A few minutes later, he stood holding two beautiful espresso drinks, one set aside. A cinnamon heart was delicately swirled onto the froth atop each, and a thin line of shaved chocolate bordered the rim of the cups. "Enjoy," he said as he handed two to Ben, then picked up his own.

"Gia!" Ben shouted into the back room. "We are about to make a job offer to someone. Wanna come out here and meet him?"

"Be right there," she called back, appearing in the doorway wiping the coffee grounds from her hands onto her apron. Ben handed Gia one of the cups, and she stared at the design, stunned. "This is beautiful!" she exclaimed. "Hi, I'm Gia." She reached out a hand toward Jet, who shook it firmly.

"Jet. Nice to meet you!" he said.

"So, Gia, it seems like Jet knows his way around an espresso bar. Would you mind covering the front for a bit so we can discuss details like hours, wages, and all that other boring stuff to see if this will work?"

"Absolutely," Gia said, leaning in to kiss Ben quickly. "No one is in the back sitting room if you want to go there. It may be more comfortable than the office. Close the door, and I'll make sure no one bothers you."

The best part of *Cold Brew* was the many nooks and crannies where customers could drink their beverages while peacefully tucked away, getting some work done, or simply enjoying the silence. The back sitting room was one of the bigger spaces and was highly sought after during the shop's busier hours. Its most desirable features were the sizeable electric fireplace set against the back wall and comfortable armchairs set before it.

Ben sat in one of the oversized chairs and gestured for Jet to take the other—and they got down to business.

A Good Night's Sleep

MORGAN

Chapter 3

THE BUS RIDE felt long as Morgan fretted about the possible repercussions of a customer complaint on her managerial prospects. Deep down, she knew Ben would probably disregard anything negative, knowing her work ethic personally, but she couldn't push the concern from her mind. She knew her boss thought she was a great barista, but what if this put into question her ability to work well—and manage—others?

She tried to sweep the negative thoughts from her mind. Finally, after several minutes, she was able to get engrossed enough in the story she was reading that it pushed the intrusive anxieties from her mind. With her nose in her book the whole time, lost in its pages, she hoped no one would disturb her for the rest of the trip.

Fortunately, the ride was quiet and uneventful. She was so

deep into the story that she almost missed her stop, realizing she needed to get off just as the bus slowed to pull up to the curb. She quickly gathered her belongings and exited with a quick wave to the driver. *That was close,* she thought. Getting off at the next stop would have taken her pretty far out of her way.

It was only a brief walk from the bus stop to Morgan's apartment—a fifth-floor walkup in an old but decently-kept building with beautiful architecture. It wasn't the best neighborhood, but it met her needs for now. It just required a bit of revitalization, she'd always said. Morgan trotted up the stairs to the front door, unlocked it, and pulled it open, then climbed several flights to her little home. Her apartment was relatively neat, except for her growing pile of laundry, mostly due to the brief amount of time she'd been there lately, primarily while sleeping. She tossed her bag on the couch and walked to the fridge, pulling it open and eyeing its contents.

"Nothing," she muttered. "Absolutely nothing." Morgan sighed and ran her hand through her sleek black hair, pushing it off her face. She had been eating most of her meals at the café lately—and sometimes Gia and Ben brought her leftovers from their restaurant. Morgan couldn't thank them enough for their kindness, but her fridge remained bare. Pulling open the freezer, she sighed. Nothing quick and easy there, either. She saw two options—order out, which didn't fit her budget, or just go to bed. She wasn't particularly hungry, anyway; she had just hoped something would catch her eye... something comforting.

Sleep, it is, Morgan thought as she left the kitchen. She opened her bedroom door and walked to the bed, crashing down upon it with her shoes still on her feet. She stared at the ceiling, trying to clear her mind, but the same images kept resurfacing: the man at the café, his voice, his eyes. Sure, he was handsome, but so were countless others who flocked in and out of the shop. Why couldn't she stop thinking about him? *You're never going to see him again. He wasn't even likable —and he may very well have robbed you of a promotion!* As her eyes grew heavy, she wasn't sure if she was asleep or awake as she imagined her hand brushing through his thick, black hair. *Cut it out, Morgan. He was a jerk!*

The next thing she knew, Morgan's eyes fluttered open as the sun's rays poured through the window. *Did I sleep all night?* she wondered. *What time is it?* She lifted her arms above her head in a deep stretch, realizing she still had her shoes on. Morgan laughed. "Guess I needed some rest," she said aloud as she glanced at the clock beside her bed. "Eleven AM—wow! Thank you, Gia and Ben."

Her cell phone lay atop the sheet next to her. She picked it up and swiped, then placed her thumb against the sensor to unlock it before reading the notifications: a few texts, one missed call—probably a bill collector—and some emails, mostly junk. She opened her texts and immediately saw one from her boss, Ben, who had sent it the evening before. *Hope that wasn't time-sensitive.*

Ben: *Hey Morgan, I hope you're asleep, but I wanted to let you know we filled the barista position. He starts training tomorrow with me. I know you probably don't want to be here on a rare day off, but if you want a coffee, please stop by to meet him. I promise I won't put you to work!*

Morgan smiled. As long as the proposed manager position's raise and schedule would allow her to pay her bills, it could allow her to re-focus on the parts of her life she'd been ignoring—like her art. She couldn't remember the last time she had picked up a pencil and paper to sketch, let alone a paintbrush. She hadn't planned to head downtown today, but her curiosity over the new hire was nagging at her. *Maybe just for a quick coffee...*

Morgan wandered over to her closet and flipped through the clothes on the hangers. *So much black,* she thought. *Cold Brew's* standard "uniform" was black. All black. Beyond that, the style was up to the individual—but the sole requirement had led to a primarily dark wardrobe since Morgan was at work most of the time. For once, she didn't want to wear 'the absence of color,' so she dug deep toward the back of the rack, sliding the black clothing further along to see what hung behind it.

"Too bright." She wrinkled her nose and pushed the almost-neon pantsuit aside. "Oof. Too tight," she said, moving a turquoise miniskirt that hadn't seen the light of day in years out of the way. "Ahh," she said, holding the sleeve of a muted floral baby-doll style dress. "Just right. It will need leggings, but... perfect." She pulled it from the hanger, laid it on the bed, and then grabbed a pair of light green capri leggings from her drawer. It was a little '90s-esque but fit well with her artsy style, and the light colors offered a nice contrast to her black hair while bringing out the light green in her eyes.

Morgan dressed quickly, brushed her hair, pinned it half back to keep it out of her eyes, and gazed in the full-length mirror. "Not bad what a little sleep can do," she said, admiring her reflection. "I may not even put any makeup on!" She glanced at the makeup on the dresser, shrugged, and walked into the living room.

Without any further primping, Morgan headed out the front door and to the bus stop. Riding public transportation in broad daylight for the second time in two days felt strange but refreshing. *The day is young, well, as young as it can be when you wake up this late,* she thought. *But first... coffee.*

Roasting

JET

Chapter 4

JET ARRIVED early to find Ben sitting on a stool before a massive coffee roaster. As the drum rotated, green coffee beans were evenly transformed to the darker brown coloring most people were accustomed to seeing. Jet had never worked in a coffee shop that roasted their beans on the premises, and the smell was incredible—like the freshest cup of coffee he could imagine, but better. It filled his nostrils with a rich, complex aroma that deepened even in the few moments since he'd started inhaling the intoxicating scent. To Jet, it was what magic would smell like!

"Wow," Jet said. "Now that's something." Ben looked up from the roaster to see Jet breathing in deeply, his eyes closed as he took in the aroma.

"Isn't it? Can't get that smell from just any coffee beans,

though." Ben watched the beans through a viewing window on the roaster.

"No?" asked Jet. "What makes them special?"

"Well," Ben began. "Every coffee type has its flavor profile depending on the variety and origin—where it comes from. Then, we can introduce further differences here through how long we roast the beans and by utilizing different processing techniques. We even mix and match different varieties to make our own unique blends. The longer you're here, the more you'll learn about roasting. You're clearly already an expert at crafting fancy drinks, and Morgan is becoming a bit of an expert coffee roaster. You'll make a great team!"

"Morgan?"

"Ah, yes. Morgan will be your co-worker. Well, technically, your manager. That's a recent development I'm still getting used to. Regardless, she's great. She could teach you about roasting, and you could probably show her a thing or two about creating those designer drinks! I never trained her on that. It's not my area of expertise! I'm more of a utilitarian coffee connoisseur."

As Ben finished his sentence, the front door swung open, and Morgan walked into *Cold Brew*. Jet could feel Morgan's eyes on him, causing him to turn toward her as she eyed him up and down.

"Ahh, speak of the devil, and she appears!" Ben said, grinning at Morgan.

"Ahh, so *this* is Morgan?" Jet asked with a slight smirk.

"In the flesh," Morgan responded somewhat coldly, tilting her head to the side.

Sensing their discomfort, Ben put one hand on each of their shoulders. "Ahh, the finest baristas in town—Morgan and Jet! Do you two, by any chance, know each other?"

"We met briefly," Jet said, a teasing smile tugging the

corners of his mouth upward. "She made me a *fabulous* drink yesterday when I stopped in for a pre-interview coffee."

"Oh! So, you checked us out before the interview, eh? I like your style. It helps to know what you're walking into beforehand. That's good business!" He could tell Morgan was still uncomfortable, so he continued to diffuse the situation. "Morgan is our star barista. She was just promoted to store manager, so I guess she'll be—uh—she will be your boss."

Ben's attempt to instill a sense of peace and calm was backfiring, and Jet and Morgan shifted their weight awkwardly, eyeing each other.

Finally, Morgan stepped toward the coffee bar. "Uh, anyway, I was just in the area running some errands. I stopped in for a quick coffee, so I'll just... I'll just go ahead and get that."

Jet stepped in front of her, effectively blocking the area behind the counter. "Please, allow me," he said. "What can I get such a marvelous barista such as yourself to fuel your errands?"

Ben patted him on the back. "Good man," he said, sitting back down in front of the coffee roaster.

"I'll take a coffee to go," Morgan said, forcing the words through clenched teeth. She was *not* pleased this would be her fellow barista and, more importantly, the man she would be managing. *He's such a cocky ass,* she thought.

"A plain coffee? Surely you want something with a little more class, a little more pizzazz."

"Just a coffee," she repeated. "Black."

Jet scoffed at the lost opportunity to show off his skills. "Alright, Boss. Whatever you say."

Morgan rolled her eyes as Jet turned around to fill a cup from the large coffee carafe behind him. Jet was excited at the opportunity to show off, even if she *did* order a plain black coffee—especially given her unwelcoming demeanor. As Jet made Morgan's beverage, he glanced at her periodically. She seemed to be looking everywhere *except* in his direction. Given the hour, there wasn't a whole lot of good "people watching" to be had, so he wasn't sure what she was even looking at. It was the middle of the day, a relatively quiet time, and there were only a few customers—some sitting with laptops open, typing away, others relaxing quietly with their caffeinated drinks and sweet treats, taking a much-needed break from their workdays.

"One boring coffee ready at the counter!" Jet said, setting the cup on the counter. He glanced down at the register, trying to determine whether it was a similar system to the one at his last job. Before he could even push any of the buttons, Ben's voice interrupted his thought process, shouting from over by the coffee roaster.

"On the house!" Ben indicated the complimentary drink to his new barista. "I don't let my baristas pay for their caffeine. They spend all day making drinks for other people... it's the least I can do!"

"Gotcha," Jet said, passing the drink to Morgan. "Hey, why don't you take the lid off and check to be sure I used the right amount of cream," he urged.

"I said *no* cream. Don't you know what black coffee means? You know what... Forget it. I'm sure it's fine," Morgan said, waving a hand dismissively. It was clear that she wanted to get out of there as quickly as possible to process this new development in her work life.

"Come on, boss. Humor me!"

Morgan sighed, rolling her eyes at his repeated use of the term "boss," and popped the top off the cup, glancing inside. At the top of her coffee, there was a stunning tree design atop a thin layer of foam. It was expertly drawn in what looked like cinnamon and chocolate syrup. Morgan tried to hide the look of surprise by keeping her eyes shifted down.

"I don't like chocolate," she mumbled.

Hearing her complaint, Ben called over, "Yes, you do."

"I don't like cinnamon, then."

"Yes... you do," Ben returned.

"Well, maybe I'm on a diet, then, Ben!" Morgan huffed, turning to glare in his direction.

"You weren't yesterday when you ate all those donuts during your shift." Ben shrugged.

Morgan knew he was only fooling around with her, but she wasn't in a good mood. She grabbed her non-black coffee, gave a quick wave and headed for the door.

"Thanks for the coffee, Ben," she called over her shoulder.

"I didn't make it."

"It's your store, isn't it? Thanks!"

Morgan left *Cold Brew* and headed for the park to enjoy her coffee in peace and maybe sketch a bit in her notebook. She had acted like a bit of a jerk, but—so had Jet!

Laundry Day

JET

Chapter 5

"JESUS CHRIST, man. What'd you do to her?" Ben stared at Jet quizzically. "She was always our nicest employee. You broke her!"

"Wasn't she your only employee?" Jet asked.

"Fair point," Ben said, rubbing his chin thoughtfully. "But she wasn't always."

"Anyway," Jet continued, "I didn't do anything, I swear. I only met her yesterday. I just suggested she rethink the foam-to-liquid ratio in the drink she made me—and to take the chocolate down a notch to let the coffee flavor shine through." Jet raised his hands up in front of him to illustrate his innocence.

Ben winced. "And... what drink was that exactly?"

Jet glanced at the menu on the wall-mounted chalkboard

to refresh his memory. His eyes scanned the offerings until they settled on one. "It was one of the ones from the artist-inspired drink menu—the Dali, I think."

"Ahh, the Artist Menu. Those are Morgan's custom creations. She's very passionate about art—and those items reflect that. We showcase the work of local and global artisans in the exhibits here at the café. We thought it'd be a cool way to get Morgan involved in another aspect of the shop before we moved her to management. She wants to go to art school, you know?"

"No, I didn't know. We just met. Anyway, I didn't know the drink was her dang pride and joy. I was only trying to help," Jet said. Then, with a grin, he added. "I certainly hope she and I can get past the disastrous first impression."

"Morgan will get over it. She's a bit moody at times, but a top-notch employee, a great barista, and a damn good friend—if you'll let her be, anyway. She's been through a lot."

"But, how is she as a manager?" Jet asked.

"It's yet to be determined. Believe it or not, she hasn't started in that capacity yet." Ben smiled. "I have a feeling she'll be just fine as long as you two can get along better than that little interaction you both just displayed."

"We'll be fine. People love me." Jet chuckled. "I'm a... people person." Jet smirked. Truth be told, he didn't like most people, but after years in the service industry, he'd become an expert at faking it. He could be as likable as anyone on Earth when it behooved him. Getting along with his manager probably fell under that category, he figured.

"I hope so. Alright, now let's get back to your training!" Ben said. "Next lesson—an introduction to the coffee roaster."

"Looking forward to it," Jet said.

"Just wait until tomorrow... That ought to be a hoot."

"What's tomorrow?"

"Barista shadowing day—with your manager," Ben said with a grin.

"Morgan," mumbled Jet, raising his hands to his head and groaning.

"Bingo!" Ben ushered Jet over to the coffee roaster, chuckling.

MORGAN

Ugh, he's such a jerk! Morgan sat on the park bench, sipping her coffee. She tried to focus on her book but quickly realized she couldn't get through more than a few pages without her mind wandering. When she realized she had re-read the same sentence a minimum of five times, she gave up. Moments later, Ben texted her to let her know that Jet would be shadowing her the next day at work to learn the ropes.

Just what I need. An arrogant punk following me around all day, giving ME pointers about MY job. She could already tell how the day was going to go, and thinking about it was giving her anxiety. She took a few deep breaths and held each for several seconds, imagining herself sitting on the shore of a lake, taking in the forest beyond. Gia, Ben's girlfriend and the co-owner of Cold Brew, had been teaching her a few visualization techniques to calm her nerves—in addition to the breathing exercises she'd learned in therapy. She was surprised to find that, used together, they actually worked for her— maybe not 100%, but they took the edge off her anxiety.

Morgan remained on the bench, deep breathing and drinking her coffee for a few more minutes before she stood, tossing her empty cup into a nearby trash can. Then, she made her way to the bus stop once again. She'd spent so much time at work lately that she was ashamed to admit how massive the pile of dirty laundry in her room was getting. "What an exciting day off work," she said to herself. "A "boring" morning coffee and an afternoon at the laundromat!"

Fortunately, *Dirty Laundry,* the local laundromat, was only about a block from where she lived. After getting off the bus, she entered her apartment and headed straight for her bedroom, where her clothes were piled into—and flowing out of—a large laundry basket in the corner. *This may take a while.* Morgan stared numbly at the pile momentarily before grabbing a massive fabric tote from her closet and the folding cart she'd purchased to make the walk to the laundromat, market, and other errands easier. It took a while, but she'd grown rather adept at a car-less life.

She began piling her clothes into the tote until it was jam-packed. *Looks like this will take a few trips... Luckily, with a new barista, I may actually have time to get things done—even if he is a jackass.* Morgan left through the door of her apartment and glanced down the stairwell. Seeing no one going up or down, she tossed the large laundry tote straight down the stairs, watching it bounce down each step, and somehow making it to the bottom without getting stuck mid-way. "Nice!" Morgan said, arriving at the last set of stairs and unfolding her cart. She stuffed the laundry bag in and began pushing it toward the building's exit, down the street toward the laundromat.

Dirty Laundry was relatively empty, given that it was still daytime during the work week. Most people were either at work or elsewhere—not doing their laundry. The machines that were running seemed abandoned by the clothing owners, likely off running errands with timers set to return when they were done. Also, *most people around here have washing machines and dryers.* Morgan knew she was lucky even to have the apartment she did, but still vowed that someday she'd have her own laundry room!

Stuffing her clothing into several different washing machines, Morgan settled into one of the chairs nearby and opened her book. As the events of earlier in the day became less fresh in her mind, she felt a little less distracted. She hoped this would allow her to focus on the story. After reading a few chapters, the timer on her phone went off, triggering her to move her laundry from the washers to the dryers.

As Morgan walked toward the dryer area, a familiar face caught her eye—jet-black hair, dark brown eyes, tall, and handsome. *Oh no. No, no, no. How is that possible?* There, standing in front of the line of dryers, was Jet. Morgan stared at the man, taking in his appearance.

It was Jet, only it wasn't. He was dressed differently—sportier—in black track pants and a torso-hugging long-sleeved shirt. His hair was swept off his face in a different style, about the same length as Jet's, but more carefully styled. Her eyes fixed on him, frozen in place, she couldn't help but wonder if she was seeing things—or losing her mind entirely from anxiety.

"Can I help you?" the man asked, realizing he was the recipient of her captive gaze and taking Morgan by surprise.

"I—uh—Do I—Do I know you? Do you know me? I—you just... You look like someone I know—just met, actually," Morgan stammered awkwardly.

"Ahh! I told him this would happen if he moved to the same town as me!" The man chuckled.

"He? Who he? He who? I mean—uhm—who's he?"

"I assume you know my brother Jethro?"

"Jethro?" Morgan narrowed her eyes for a moment, confused. "Oh, Jet, yes! I thought you were him for a moment. Is he your brother?" After the words left her mouth, she realized it was probably a dumb question. They were obviously twins—maybe not identical twins, but *very* alike in their appearance. Similar to the point that it'd be easy to confuse one for the other if their style was more similar. *Twins?!* Morgan thought to herself. *You don't meet twin brothers in two different locations on the same day—that type of thing only happens in books!*

"Ah, still going by Jet to those who didn't grow up with us, I see. We get that a lot. Twins, but we do our best to make ourselves distinguishable from one another. Sometimes it works." He stopped to gesture at Gia as an example. "And sometimes it doesn't. I'm Jace. No ridiculous nickname—just Jace."

Morgan couldn't help but continue to stare at this man whose personality seemed so opposite from his arrogant, cocky brother. "I'm Morgan."

"A pleasure to meet you, Morgan. And how, may I ask, do you know my bonehead brother?"

"Well," Morgan began, "I will be his manager starting tomorrow morning.

Lost

MORGAN

Chapter 6

Jace rolled his eyes. "About time he got a real job since moving here. As good as he is, admittedly, the band thing doesn't pay the rent. It's time for little Jethro to grow up. Where is little bro going to be working, anyway?"

"Little? I thought you were twins?"

"I came out first—and I'm much more mature." Jace grinned at Morgan as she loaded her clean laundry into the dryer.

"I don't think it would take much," said Morgan, rolling her eyes.

"Ahh, my brother... ever the hero of first impressions. Not smart to piss off your manager before you even start the job, is it?" Jace's tone seemed flirty, and Morgan felt herself drawn to him. She was compelled to flirt back for the first time in a long time!

"No, it's not. Now, tell me... Do you really want to know where your brother works, or are you trying to find out where *I* work for personal reasons?" Before she even knew what she was saying, the rather forward words flew from her lips. *Did I just say that out loud?* Morgan winced at the sheer boldness of the flirtation.

"I'd be lying if I said I wasn't at least somewhat intrigued," Jace said with a smile that Morgan returned.

"*Cold Brew on Main*," she revealed. "The coffee shop."

"Ahh, makes sense for Jethro. Barista to the bone. You too?"

"Yep," Morgan started, then paused a moment, thinking. "Coffee is pretty much all I know how to do beyond my art, which I haven't had much time for lately. Tomorrow's my first day as a manager, though, and my first day working with your brother." Morgan put her head in her hands and groaned.

"Well, truth be told, he's not so bad. Don't tell him I said that. We don't always get along. He's a bit of an acquired taste and doesn't have much of a filter. But, at least with him, what you see is what you get." Jace shrugged and gestured to the chairs just beyond the line of dryers. "Want to sit? My stuff's not done yet. It may take longer than yours, actually—comforters and whatnot."

"Sure," Morgan said, sitting in one of the chairs as Jace sat beside her.

The conversation flowed freely until Morgan's dryer completed its cycle. Jace told her about his job as some kind of a sports agent, pulling out his wallet to display several pictures of himself standing next to some apparently famous athletes. Not particularly big on sports, he could have told her a group of professional ping-pong players were NFL football players and she wouldn't have been any the wiser. She listened intently as he talked, taking in the many stark contrasts between him and his brother.

When the alarm on her phone alerted her to check it, she opened the machine and felt the clothes inside. They were dry. *Oh well, leave 'em wanting more, I guess.* Morgan began unloading the dryer and shoving her clothes into the laundry bag. She'd fold when she got home. Something about having her clothes laid out on full display to Jace while she was folding made her feel awkward.

"Well, this is my cue to leave," she called. "I have a potentially very long workday in store tomorrow with your bratty little brother under my wing," she teased.

"Fair enough. Hey, can I have your number?" Jace asked, grinning. "Or is that weird since you're my twin's manager?"

"It's probably a little weird, but I won't say no..." Morgan reached into her bag and pulled out a colored pencil she'd brought along in case the urge to sketch struck at any time during her day off. Then, she ripped a sheet of paper from her sketchbook and jotted down her phone number. "Here. Feel free to call or text—but I'm more of a texter."

Unwilling to stick around for an awkward goodbye, Morgan turned and wheeled her cart out the laundromat door, failing to see a small article of clothing drop from her bag to the floor right at Jace's feet.

When she arrived back at her apartment, Morgan had a quick snack of stale tortilla chips before sitting on her bed with her clean laundry sprawled around her. Her mind wandered as she folded, making piles of shirts, pants, and underwear to allow her to put the clothes away in their rightful locations more easily. Fortunately, the more positive interaction with Jace had taken over her thoughts, replacing those of his brother at the coffee shop—and somewhat easing the sense of dread that came over her every time she thought about going to work the next day. She was pulled back to the present by the quick vibration of the phone beside her. It was a text message.

Hey! It's Jace. I wanted to give you my number, too. It was a pleasure meeting you today. I'd like to see you again. Maybe I'll stop into Cold Brew tomorrow? I actually have something for you.

Morgan's lips turned up into a smile. It *was* a pleasure. Her happiness at hearing from him so quickly turned to confusion. *What could he possibly have for me? We just met!* Not wanting to appear too curious, she lifted the phone and began to type a response:

Hi, Jace. Good to hear from you. I'd like that. I'll be there all day, starting at 5 a.m. Ew.

She hit send on the message and returned to her laundry, embarrassingly giddy over the thought of seeing someone she had only met once. *I guess I'll just have to wait until tomorrow to see what he has for me. I wonder what Jet will think when his brother shows up to see me.* She didn't want it to be awkward, but she couldn't help but wonder if being friends—or more—with Jace would give her some ammo that could come in handy as his manager.

Morgan pulled out her favorite black pants from the pile and laid them out for the next day. They hugged her legs in all the right places, from hip to calf, and she had always thought they made her behind look far more toned than it really was.

She searched through the yet-to-be-folded pile. *Perfect.* Morgan pulled out a flowing black two-layer shirt. The first layer was a tank top that highlighted her curves, while the sheer top layer toned it down, covering her arms in bell-style sleeves and making it more appropriate for work. She thanked her lucky stars that she had finally done her laundry and had options! Then, she grabbed a black bra and—

"Wait. Where are my favorite panties?" she said aloud.

They weren't pretty—full-coverage hipsters that could be considered "granny panties" by most accounts—but they were functional, didn't give her a wedgie, and were thin enough not to show through her pants. *Maybe they didn't make it to the laundry bag, somehow. I bet they're around here somewhere. Oh well.*

Morgan knew she was far from organized lately, so it was entirely possible that they were strewn somewhere around the apartment, possibly under her bed. She dug through the pile and grabbed a different pair, adding it to her outfit for the next day and setting the garments on her dresser. She'd grown accustomed to laying her clothes out at night, so they'd be easy to grab at 4 a.m. before work when she was still half asleep. *Ahh, the life of a barista!*

... *And Found*

JET

Chapter 7

JET WALKED UP to the entrance of *Cold Brew on Main* and turned the handle of the front door to let himself in for his first day of official employment at the establishment. Upon realizing the doors were locked, he cupped his hands to either side of his head and peered inside the window. He saw it was still dark inside and glanced at his watch. *Tsk, tsk, Morgan. You're late.*

Jet sat on the curb in front of the building and waited. He pulled the guitar strapped across his back off and began quietly strumming chords until his phone vibrated in his pocket. Taking it out, he saw a notification of unread messages in the group chat with his bandmates. He scrolled upward, scanning the conversation. After confirming their schedule for the following week worked for him, the topic turned to his first day at his new job. Somehow, it then shifted to his boss. He wasn't exactly sure how he began by discussing how much of a pain in his ass Morgan was already and finished by admitting how hot she was, but what else could he say? They asked, and she *was* hot.

Within a few minutes, he saw the silhouette of a woman wearing all black walking down Main Street toward the café. She was thin but had incredible curves. Just his type. As she drew closer, he saw that her hair was pulled back, a few wavy tendrils framing her face. *Stunning,* he thought. Then, he focused in on the face—Morgan.

He tucked his phone back in his pocket and shook his head back and forth a few times to recover from the fact that he had totally been checking out his new boss. *Come on, Jet. What the hell, man? She hates you, anyway!* Morgan arrived at the front of the building and glanced down at Jet, who jumped to his feet clumsily, still holding his guitar. He recovered quickly. "You're late," he said, smirking at Morgan.

"Good morning, Jethro." Morgan enunciated the last word, smirking. "Sometimes the bus has issues." She rolled her eyes. "I could open this place in about 45 seconds if I had to."

"It's Jet," Jet grumbled. "Ben told you my full name? Jackass. And, is that a fact?"

"It is," said Morgan as she inserted her key and maneuvered it to unlock the front door. "And, *lucky for me,* now I have help!" She raised her eyebrows at Jet as she walked into *Cold Brew,* switched the lights on, and headed behind the counter to set up for the morning rush. "You coming?" she asked Jet over her shoulder.

He entered and followed the same path as Morgan to the back. As he was removing his black leather jacket and hanging it on the hooks in the storage room, the doorbell to the back door rang. "Oh, that's the bakery delivery. Can you just open the door and let them in? They know what to do," Morgan directed. Jet nodded and walked toward the back of the store to accept the delivery, which was carried in and placed near the baked goods display.

Morgan was grateful that the early morning hours were always a rush of activity to get the store open and ready for the morning commuter chaos. It took her mind off the fact that she had to work with Jet. She began loading the baked goods from their boxes onto the trays in the display case, explaining to Jet where each type of pastry went as she put them away. When they'd finished setting up the food, Morgan asked him to brew the morning's regular, non-espresso coffee selections.

"Choose one decaf, a dark brew, and a medium to light brew. Those will be the coffees of the day—we change it up to let people try different types of coffee if they want, but we always have our store brew available for those who don't like to switch it up. So, you'll be brewing four types of coffee but doing two of each—so, eight carafes worth—because it goes quickly during the morning rush. Having an extra one brewed and ready to go is essential." Morgan pointed to the line of clean carafes sitting on the counter waiting. "After they're filled, they sit two-by-two on that counter, and the coffee labels get inserted into the slots in the carafes. Also, we write the types available on the Coffee of the Day chalkboard near the entrance."

"You do know I've done this before, correct?" Jet asked.

"Yes, but not here. We do things differently here. It's—it's —special." Morgan felt silly after saying it and all the more so after hearing Jet's response.

"It's a coffee shop. As special as you may think it is, you make the coffee and then give people the coffee. That's its purpose, and that's really all you need to know to work in it. Oh, and learning the drink recipes, but that's just simple memorization—and most people don't even know what they're ordering. I can steam milk and run espresso shots in my sleep."

Morgan scoffed. "*Cold Brew* is so much more than that. Ben poured his heart and soul into this place when he took over, and Gia, too, once she and Ben got together. They care about their employees and the community, and this little coffee shop has a global impact, too. Here." She shoved a brochure at Jet detailing the rainforest communities *Cold Brew* networked with to establish fair-trade relationships and to provide locals with jobs, education, skills training, and more."

"Okay, okay. Maybe it's a *bit* different," Jet conceded, glancing at the clock. "Ten minutes before opening. What else do we need to do, Boss?"

Morgan gazed around the store. Ben had pre-prepped the garbage cans with bags at closing the night before, for which she was grateful. "Really, we just need to put the creamers, sweeteners, and flavored syrups out at the self-prep area for those who like to do it themselves, and then we can open."

As the clock struck 6 a.m., Morgan walked over to the door and flipped a sign hanging beside it from closed to open. As she turned on her heel to head back behind the counter, her eyes caught something through the window, and she gasped.

"You okay over there?" Jet asked.

"Yeah, I—uh—I," she stammered.

"Spit it out, Boss Lady! You look like you're staring at a ghost."

Morgan gestured to the door as it was opening—and there stood Jace. He wore a burgundy tracksuit with white and black striping and held a sports bag over his shoulder. She hadn't entirely expected him to come at all, let alone to be the very first customer of the day—at precisely 6 a.m. *He looks like an advertisement for an athletics company.* Morgan ran a hand through her hair, smoothing it.

"Good morning, everyone! And how is our first day working together going?" Jace asked, a wide grin forming.

"Jace, what are you doing here? How did you know I was —" Jet was interrupted mid-sentence.

"Oh, Jethro, Jethro, Jethro—a little bird told me you were starting work here today. A very pretty little bird, I may add," Jace said, winking at Morgan. Morgan blushed and looked down, suddenly embarrassed that she hadn't mentioned that they had met the day before. It just hadn't come up.

"You two know each other?" Jet asked.

"We just met," Morgan quickly answered, feeling even more uncomfortable.

It was strange seeing the twin brothers side-by-side. They were both startlingly handsome and shared the same dark hair and eyes. Jace was a little larger, especially in his chest and arms, likely from mornings at the gym judging from his attire, while Jet was a more artsy musician type. It was unlikely that he spent a significant amount of time at the gym, but he was still tall and appeared strong.

"Would you like some coffee?" Morgan asked, snapping out of the daze she had briefly fallen into while comparing the two men in her head and changing the subject.

"I'd love some. Thanks." As Jace moved past Morgan toward the counter to place his order and pay, he stealthily slipped something into Morgan's hand. As she glanced down at her fist, she clenched it tighter, and her jaw dropped. *My panties!* she realized, absolutely mortified.

As she looked up, she saw the grin on Jace's face. He took a few steps back toward her and whispered, "Our little secret," giving her a wink.

MORGAN

Morgan shoved the balled-up underwear into her pocket, her cheeks turning several shades pinker. As she moved awkwardly past Jace to make his coffee, he whispered, "You're cute when you blush," causing the color to deepen even more.

"I—uh—what type of drink would you like?" Morgan gestured to the menu as she caught a glimpse of Jet's confused expression out of the corner of her eye. She wasn't sure how much of the interaction between her and his brother he had seen, if any.

"Hmm," Jace said, rubbing his chin thoughtfully. "What would you recommend?"

"Depends on what you like—sweet, bold, dark, light?" Morgan asked.

"Light, sweet, and creamy—just like how I like my women."

Morgan was taken aback momentarily. Both from his comment and by the fact that she wasn't usually wrong when she made assumptions about people's coffee preferences—but she had been with Jace. She liked her coffee dark and strong, with no cream or sugar most of the time. For some reason, she'd assumed the same about him. *To each his own,* she thought, reaching for the steam wand. "How about a Da Vinci's Dream? It's a dirty latte with chocolate syrup, a touch of sweet cream cold foam, topped with chocolate shavings. Very—uh—" Morgan paused, searching for the right word. "Decadent."

"Perfect." Jace nodded and turned sideways to lean against the counter while Jet stood toward the opposite side of the back area, taking in the interaction between the two and rolling his eyes. "So, what makes it... dirty?" Jace asked, clearly flirting and laying it on thick. It almost seemed like he was intentionally trying to make Jet uncomfortable.

Morgan stumbled over her words again, her mind wandering from espresso beverages momentarily. "Uh, it's uhm—well—the coffee poured over the milk makes it a 'dirty' color, I guess." Morgan desperately hoped she looked significantly less awkward than she felt. *Not the most glamorous explanation, but it's the truth.*

Jace leaned against the counter, allowing him to get closer to Morgan as she poured the espresso shots over the cold milk. She lifted the cup to hold it into the light, and, as promised, the layers of milk and espresso combined somewhat, making a 'muddy' colored beverage. "Gotcha. Well, now that we've met twice and you've made me a dirty drink, would it be appropriate to ask you to dinner?"

Taken by surprise, Morgan abruptly shifted her weight, bumping her elbow against the baked goods case and practically dropping the dirty latte. Instead, out of nowhere, Jet appeared, grabbing the drink with one hand while steadying her with the other. He glanced at Jace, raised an eyebrow, and handed him the beverage.

"If you're done distracting my manager, can we get back to work here, please?" He held the cup out toward his brother, still holding Morgan's shoulder with one hand.

"We were just finishing our conversation, weren't we, Morgan?" Jace channeled all his masculine charm into the smile he flashed at Morgan, causing her knees to weaken. For a moment, she was glad Jet was still holding onto her, or she may have fallen right over. She was, however, surprised at how strong his hand felt on her shoulder.

"Yes, I—uh—I'll text you later, okay?" Morgan said, sensing a strange distance between the two brothers and feeling uncomfortable responding to Jace's question in any more detail in front of Jet.

"Alright, I can accept that. I'm off to the gym. You two kids be good!" Jace said as he walked toward the exit, tossing a quick wave over his shoulder as he pulled open the door and left *Cold Brew*. After he had cleared the door, Morgan turned to stare at Jet.

"You can let go now," she said, bringing her hand up toward her shoulder and removing Jet's hand. "What the hell was that? You barely said two words to each other. What's with you two?"

"We don't really get along all that well," Jet started. "And, if you know what's good for you, you'd steer clear of Jace, too. He isn't all that he makes himself out to be."

"What do you mean?"

"It's just... he wouldn't be good for you. Or anyone, really. It's easy to fall for his charm, but Jace only thinks about Jace. He's bad news. Really bad news." Jet began walking toward the cash register, where a short line had formed in the few moments since his brother had left. "Better get moving. You know as well as I do that this line will only grow through rush hour!"

Morgan was curious about what could make the twin brothers so cold toward one another, but Jet was right. The line was quickly building, and she was supposed to be managing things—instead, she had been flirting. Jet was already an experienced barista, and since the drink recipes were marked on a 'cheat sheet' by the espresso machine, Morgan could handle the cash register and take orders while he prepared the beverages.

She had gotten used to handling both processes on her own, jumping back and forth, so with the extra set of hands, they made light work out of the line and caught things up quickly. The rest of the morning was busy, as always, but nothing Morgan couldn't handle—especially with the extra help. She spent the hours chatting with her regulars, introducing the new staff member to customers, taking food and drink orders, and teaching Jet the basics of how to run the shop.

She had almost forgotten about her morning interactions with Jace until the chaos died down around mid-morning, and her phone began buzzing. *Text message.* Morgan pulled her phone out and glanced at the screen. It was Jace.

Jace: *Hey Coffee Cutie. Great choice on the drink this morning. I guess I like my coffee dirty, too. Who knew? You never gave me an answer about dinner. What do you think?*

Morgan felt her cheeks heating up, remembering his comment about liking his coffee like his women. She glanced at Jet, who was wiping down the barista bar with a towel, then looked at her phone again. Working with Jet hadn't been nearly as bad as she had expected. He was quick to make the drinks, a good listener, and a fast learner. All in all, it had been one of her most effortless mornings at work in recent memory. The rush was easier to handle when someone else could jump in and keep things moving.

"Hey, Jet?" she said.

"Yes, ma'am?" he joked, implying again that she was the boss.

"Just Morgan. For the love of coffee—just Morgan! 'Boss' makes me feel like I'm in the mob, and 'ma'am' makes me feel old!"

"Okay, okay, Morgan, it is. Until I find something better, anyway," he said, smirking.

"So," Morgan began, "what's really up with you and your brother?"

"It's a long story. A bit of ancient history, regrettable and not easily forgettable."

"Were you ever close?"

"We used to be. We are just very different, I guess you could say." Jet paused for a minute over the sink, rinsing, then ringing out a towel. "And yet we have a history of sharing the same taste in women." Jet looked down toward his feet to avoid Morgan's gaze. "Oh, not you. I didn't mean you!" he added awkwardly.

Morgan couldn't help but notice his expression was briefly stricken with unmistakable sadness when she'd asked about his relationship with his brother. "Oh," she said, realizing that perhaps a woman had come between them. "I see."

"Anyway, again, it's a long and very personal story. But take it from me: Jet's not good for *anyone*. Do with that what you will—but don't say I didn't warn you. I know he can be very charming... Oh, look, customers! Moving on..." Jet chuckled, seemingly happy to abruptly end the conversation.

Saved by the insatiable draw of caffeine, thought Morgan.

Matt & Carla's Cameo

JET

Chapter 8

HE'S SUCH AN ASS. Jet kept the words housed within his mind despite wanting desperately to pour them out in a torrent of anger. *He's ALWAYS there.* Jet knew that by moving to the area, he would run the risk of seeing his twin brother. Still, he always appeared at the most inopportune times, behaving obnoxiously. Today, for example—on his first day at a new job. Hitting on his manager.

Jet had to maintain his cool, though. He wouldn't let Jace's arrogance get to him. They had agreed to leave the past behind them and to see each other only when absolutely necessary, recognizing that a deep rift had formed between them. It was a chasm that Jet would never allow to close entirely... not after what he had done. He wanted to tell Morgan to delete his number, block him, and get as far away from him as possible to avoid the inevitable heartache that *any* woman—or any person—who came in contact with Jace wound up experiencing.

It wasn't his place, though. Not yet, anyway. He barely knew her, and Jet was fairly confident she hated him despite a relatively pain-free morning working together. Sure, he hoped she wouldn't have to learn about Jace the hard way, but he'd warned her! He was in no position to go into all the details when he was still trying to forget them himself. Jet pushed away the triggering thoughts that had begun creeping into his mind and threw himself into the workday. He focused his attention elsewhere by memorizing the coffee drinks, learning the point-of-sale system on the register, and familiarizing himself with the routines and procedures at the café.

Jet was a model employee, even as far as Morgan was concerned, it seemed. Since Jace had left earlier that morning, she hadn't made one snide remark about how he emptied the garbage or tapped his espresso shots. In a way, it was throwing him off. Judging from their prior interactions, he'd been prepared for her to keep him on his toes—but she seemed pretty chill.

"So, I was gonna ask if your parents had named you Jet—I thought that was pretty cool—but your brother kind of threw you under the bus there, Jethro," Morgan said, interrupting his thoughts to tease him.

Jet winced. "He's a dick for telling you that. And here I was, blaming Ben! Yeah, I took a lot of grief for the name Jethro as a kid. Around high school, my then-girlfriend started shortening it to Jet, and it kind of just stuck. It works for the band and whatnot, too. Jet on guitar sounds a whole lot cooler than Jethro." He waved toward where his guitar was still leaning against a wall in the back room.

"What's your band's name anyway?" Morgan asked as she swept a pile of spilled coffee grounds off the counter and into the trash with a small brush. They were coming into the first lull of the day, and while several patrons were seated around the coffee shop, there was no line for beverages. Jet glanced at her sideways as if weighing his response carefully.

"Promise not to laugh?"

"Why would I laugh? Is it that bad?"

"I mean... it's not great." Jet grinned, putting his hand against his face. "The Degenerate Dinosaurs."

"The—Degenerate—Dinosaurs? The Degenerate Dinosaurs. It's, uh..." Morgan searched for the right words but came up speechless. "It's..."

"You should see your face right now!" Jet said, laughter escaping in waves from somewhere deep within. "You are trying *so* hard to be nice and coming up blank. Completely empty-handed." His expression seemed somehow gentler than it had in their previous interactions despite his teasing tone. "Relax. We are actually called The Plot Twists, which I also don't love, but it's better than Degenerate Dinosaurs, right?"

"Oh my God, I didn't know what to say." Morgan slapped her hand against her forehead in a face-palm motion. "It was *so* bad—so, SO bad! I really do like the name The Plot Twists, though. I'm a big reader, so it works for me. Reminds me of books." She wiped the counter with a damp rag, then continued, "What type of music? And I assume you play guitar?"

"Like the name, we try to change things up and surprise listeners with an eclectic mix of genres and storytelling through music and lyrics. I sing and play guitar. We all sing, though. It's not a typical frontman setup." Jet grabbed another rag and started wiping down the espresso machine while Morgan began to brew another pot of coffee.

"What's your most well-known song?"

"That would probably be *Twist of Fate*, although I

45

wouldn't exactly call it well-known. It starts slow and ballad-like but finishes as a much harder, heavier rock song. Our music's sound and lyrics are... kind of... hard to explain. It's about the contrasts in life, but how they're all important—hard, soft, light, dark. It all matters."

"What's *Twist of Fate* about? You said storytelling, so what's the story behind it?" Morgan looked at Jet curiously, her interest appearing sincere.

"Well, it follows a few different individuals and several chance encounters that change their lives—some for better, others for worse, but all in an instant and beyond their control. It tells their stories and ties them together at the end."

"That sounds unique. I like that. Do you have an album recorded?"

"We have a few songs recorded as demos, but we only really started to get them down as tracks when I moved closer to the other guys, so we're just getting started."

A customer walked up to the counter, requesting a to-go cup for a coffee they had started drinking in the café earlier. Jet paused to help before continuing the conversation. "Meeting regularly for band practice, recording sessions, and whatnot before was just too hard with the guys all living together and me in another town. We were gaining popularity in the local music scene, but things were dragging regarding scheduling appearances and getting into the studio together. Ultimately, it came down to me moving closer or leaving the band. So—here I am."

"Well, it seems to be working out for you so far," Morgan said, glancing at the clock to assess how much time remained in the workday and whether they could get started on any closing procedures early. "New job, closer to your family—your brother, anyway—and evenings free for gigs and recording sessions. Indie coffee shop hours suck in some, okay, many ways, but they work out well in others. We aren't open as late as some of the corporate caffeine spots. Those early mornings, though. Oof."

"You're telling me. This isn't my first rodeo, remember? And as for my brother and me, well, like I said, that's a long story. I don't think of being closer to him as a benefit. More like a necessary evil."

Morgan could tell it wasn't a subject he wanted to discuss further, so she returned to the relatively safe topic of work. "Well, you've picked up how we do things around here really quickly. Don't get used to hearing it, but I'm impressed," Morgan joked, smiling at Jet as the door swung open, and two of *Cold Brew's* regular customers, who also happened to be friends with the shop owners, appeared. Morgan always tried to make a good impression on Carla and Matt, knowing they'd pass on a report of their experience to Ben and Gia. Plus, they were just good people.

The tall, well-built male wrapped his arm around his pretty wife's waist, tucking his hand conveniently into her back left jean pocket. She jokingly ran in through the door a little bit ahead of him, feigning weakness while moaning, "Caffeine! Must—have—caffeine! Parched! Matt didn't tell me we ran out of coffee." She pretended to faint. "And we only have... *decaf!* Who even drinks decaf coffee?! What's the point? It's sacrilege!"

Matt glanced at his wife and rolled his eyes. "Everyone, ignore Carla. She will, in fact, survive the horrible abuse I've subjected her to. And for the record, we *do* have caffeinated coffee. It's just hazelnut-flavored. God forbid."

"Coffee is meant to be *coffee*-flavored. No nuts in the morning," Carla muttered.

"Carla, my love, *you're* the only nut around here. Alright. Hello, *Cold Brew* staff. Let's start over!" Matt grinned at the two baristas behind the counter. "Good morning, Morgan. Hey, new guy. Ben mentioned you were starting today. How badly is Morgan torturing you?" Matt asked.

"Maaaatttt! First coffee, then talky." Carla prodded Matt in the ribs, whining.

"Ugh. Fine. Two coffees. One light and sweet with cream. One black." Matt stopped momentarily and rested a hand against the side of his face to cover his mouth from Carla. "... Like her heart and soul!" he fake-whispered.

"You'd be soulless, too, if you had to wake up without coffee," Carla scoffed.

"Two coffees, coming right up!" Jet grabbed two cups. "What kind?"

"Anything but hazelnut! Ben always says the Brazilian brew is the best, so we usually go with that," Carla said. "It's delicious. Even when I'm watching my calories, and I have to drink it black. You know, *like my soul*." She stuck out her tongue, making a raspberry sound at her husband.

Jet grinned, getting a kick out of Carla and Matt's interactions. They were a feisty couple, but it was clear that it was all good fun. Matt's hand hadn't left its location in Carla's back pocket the entire time, and she didn't seem to mind.

"Two Brazilian brews with absolutely NO hazelnut or any other nuts—all set." Jet handed the coffees to Matt and Carla.

"Thanks, oh—still didn't catch your name," Matt said.

"Oh, it's Jet."

"Jethrooooo," Morgan added, then ducked behind the bakery case, giggling.

Jet smirked. "Just Jet." He kicked his foot at Morgan behind the scones, where she was still crouched.

"All right, just Jet and Morgan, thanks for the coffee. See you two around!"

Crystal

MORGAN

Chapter 9

MORGAN WAVED goodbye to Carla and Matt as they left the café. "That's Carla and Matt," Morgan said, regretting the words the moment they left her mouth.

"Yeah, I kinda got that." Jet grinned. "Given that they said it and all."

"Right. Oh yeah. Anyway, they come in a lot. Pretty basic orders, usually. They live next to Gia, and they've known her and Ben forever, at least since high school, maybe before. I think Carla and Matt somehow got them back together after Gia's divorce, but I don't know the whole story. They all went to Brazil relatively recently to visit the site where the coffee we use for our Brazilian blend comes from. Ben owns an eco-resort paired with a sustainable, fair-trade coffee business. It

49

was the first site he worked on, long before becoming some high-demand global eco-tourism guru."

Morgan realized she was rambling and reigned herself in, stopping herself from talking by taking a swig of the Mint Zing iced tea she had prepared for herself. You can only drink so much coffee in a day before your hands start to shake and you switch to herbal teas—or at least break it up with a decaf in between.

"Wow. That's awesome." Jet appeared to be genuinely interested, which made Morgan relax a little. "That's what I like about this place over the big chains, I guess," he continued. "It has stories attached. People and their stories... In case you hadn't noticed with the band and whatnot, I'm big on stories."

"I told you *Cold Brew* was different. Speaking of stories, do you read at all?"

"Ironic, isn't it? Not much. I used to all the time, but I haven't had much time lately between work and the band—and the travel between. Maybe now that I'm closer to everything, I'll be able to pull off a few more books this year—like, more than zero, perhaps."

"It's funny because my travel time is when I *do* read."

"Audiobooks?" Jet asked.

"Nope. Just reading on the bus."

"Ahh, you don't drive?"

"Nope. Long story." After meeting Jet for less than a complete shift, Morgan wasn't prepared to discuss her financial circumstances in detail, so she hoped he would change the subject.

"Fair enough—although, as I said, I do love a good story."

"Maybe some other time." Morgan shifted her weight awkwardly and glanced out the door, hoping someone would walk in sooner rather than later. Just as the thought crossed her mind, the door opened, and a noisy crowd of teenagers entered. She glanced at the clock. *Ahh, high school dismissal.*

Cold Brew was within walking distance of the local high school and had become the habitual after-school hangout of a bevy of artsy types, from musicians to writers. Not that it wasn't frequented by the other crowds as well, but the artists tended to gravitate toward the caffeine hub in larger droves as a place to hang out. The athletes popped in for a coffee, then left. *Ahh, stereotypes.*

The artsy crowd reminded Morgan a lot of herself as a teen, though, and she enjoyed their presence. She even kept tabs on how fast her shift was progressing by their arrivals and departures. Sometimes, the morning flew by—other times, by the time they appeared, she couldn't believe she still had several hours of work left!

Working extra shifts and tag-teaming with Ben and Gia to cover the café's business hours certainly wasn't making the days feel any shorter—but she hoped that would change with Jet's hiring. She couldn't help but notice the morning had flown by in his presence despite moments of uncomfortable silence and dwindling conversation here and there. Overall, it'd been pleasant.

Morgan glanced at the door, examining the faces as they entered to see who was in the group before calling out drink orders to Jet. For as unique and one-of-a-kind as these kids were, they were certainly predictable when it came to their choice of caffeinated beverages. In all her time working at *Cold Brew,* their orders hadn't changed once that she could recall. She'd taken to prepping the drinks as soon as she saw the kids appear. This was as good a time as any to show off her deep knowledge of her customers to Jet—and to prove that *Cold Brew* wasn't just any old coffee shop.

"One DaVinci's Dream, two Picassos on Ice, a black iced

coffee—light on the ice, a hot coffee—light and sweet with cream and sugar, a—"

"Easy, killer!" Jet interrupted. "Can you write it on the cups?"

Morgan stared at Jet. "We don't... We don't do that here."

"Well, maybe you should," Jet said, shrugging his shoulders. "One at a time. I don't know these drink names the way you do yet."

Morgan nodded, realizing, perhaps, she had been working on her own for a bit too long. "Sorry. Start with the DaVinci, then the regular coffee and iced. I've got the Picassos." Morgan smiled at Jet, trying to appear understanding. *He's not trying to slow me down. He's just new—and all things considered, he's quite good.*

Jet got to work preparing the drinks he'd been assigned while Morgan worked on hers, introducing her new coworker to the group of high schoolers as she steamed the milk.

Morgan brought the drinks to the register area one by one, just as a tall, thin brunette with dark makeup and long braids on each side leaned in and whispered, "Is he single?" Morgan was taken by surprise, and she almost dropped the cup she was holding out to the girl.

"I—what?"

"The new barista—he's hot. Is he dating anyone?"

"Crystal, I just met him. I'm not really sure. Isn't he a little too old for you, anyway?" Morgan glanced at the high school girl, trying to assess her age—and legality.

"Age is just a number," Crystal said, winking.

Morgan chuckled. "Tell that to law enforcement. I think their opinion on the matter may differ."

"Yeah... Maybe." Crystal grinned at her. "What they don't know won't hurt them, will it? Anyway, I'll be eighteen in a few weeks."

Morgan kept her eyes on the younger girl, glad they had

developed enough of a rapport that she could at least let her true feelings on the matter show to some degree. As Morgan and Jet finished making the drinks and rang up the kids, Crystal leaned over the bar toward Jet, batting her eyelashes.

"So, Jet... Welcome. What brings you to *Cold Brew?*" she cooed, causing him to take a step back, clearly uncomfortable.

Not to appear rude, especially to customers, Jet smiled at Crystal. "Moved to town recently. Had to get a real job sooner or later, you know? Bills and all that!"

"New in town, huh? Interesting." Crystal sipped slowly from the rim of her drink, taking a long sip, then licking her lips, clearly trying to shift his focus to her mouth. "Well, you certainly know how to make a good espresso drink. I wonder what else you can do for a girl." She dipped her finger into the foam on top of her beverage and seductively brought it to her lips, tracing her tongue in a circle around her finger suggestively.

Having just sipped his own beverage, Jet started coughing —spewing coffee from his mouth. "I, uh... Hey Morgan, I need to go do that thing you asked me to do in the back. Right now. Morgan? Can you take over?" Jet wiped the coffee from the corners of his mouth and dabbed his wet shirt with a towel. He looked desperate for an escape, and Morgan didn't miss it.

"You got it," Morgan said, gesturing to the back. "I'll come check on those inventory numbers shortly." Morgan tilted her head to the side and shifted her eyes back to Crystal, narrowing them. "Stop screwing around with my staff," she said.

"While I'd certainly love to be doing that, that's not all I'd like to be doing with your staff..." Crystal trailed off, her eyes wandering to follow Jet's silhouette as he walked to the back of the building.

It's a Date

JET

Chapter 10

JET STUMBLED toward the back room, still sputtering on the coffee he'd spewed all over himself only moments before. He was used to being hit on. It was par for the course when you were in a band—lots of bar gigs, flowing alcohol, not so much inhibition—but she was *young*. "No, thank you," he muttered to himself. "I have enough problems as it is!"

When he reached the supply room, he began counting the unopened boxes of napkins and to-go cups. It gave him something to do until he knew the coast was clear. It was on his task list for the shift anyway. Finally, after what felt like forever, he heard footsteps heading in his direction. "Jet? You still back here? They left," Morgan said. "It's safe!"

"Thank goodness," Jet began. "She's gone? Promise?"

"She's gone. But she'll be back. She's a regular. You'll have to figure out how to deal with that one. *She's almost eighteen, after all.*" Morgan grinned at Jet, emphasizing the last sentence to tease him. Her face softened as she added, "Crystal is harmless, I think. She's just looking for something to help her get through. She had a rough breakup a few months ago, and she hasn't really been the same since. Sadder—a little darker—so, be gentle however you decide to deal with that mess."

"I will. Despite emotional stupidity being a common trend in many men, I don't suffer from it," Jet said, glancing at Morgan, who appeared surprised by his response.

The remainder of the afternoon passed without any further events of note. Morgan introduced Jet to several of the other daily *Cold Brew* customers, and he hit it off well with them. He worked on memorizing the drink names, ingredients, and prep when it was slow, and by the time the evening rush came through—primarily commuters heading home for the day— he could make most of the beverages without even glancing at his cheat sheet.

When they finally flipped the door sign to *closed*, Jet was exhausted. His senses were overloaded by the slew of new people, new drinks, new procedures, and so on. They moved quickly to wipe down the counters, change the garbage bags, and clean the bathrooms, trying to get out of there as early as possible. Once things settled down, only one of them would stay for the evening closing based on a pre-set schedule—but Jet was still in training.

"It sure makes the evening cleanup faster having a second person to close with!" Morgan declared as they each carried a garbage bag to the dumpster behind the building.

"I'll bet," Jet said, lifting his bag over the dumpster's rim, tossing it in, and reaching for Morgan's bag. She handed it over, and he threw it in and closed the top.

"Thanks," Morgan said, smiling.

"You know," Jet began. "I thought I was going to hate you, but you aren't too bad so far—even saved me from the jailbait fangirl."

"Funny," Morgan said. "I felt the same way. And, so far, I've been pleasantly surprised. Now, don't mess it up!" Morgan laughed as Jet pulled the heavy back door open. "And, with that said, you're free to go! We're officially off-duty until tomorrow. And my bus arrives in six minutes, so I've gotta jet." A smirk crossed her face as she realized her unintentional use of his name. "No pun intended."

Jet grinned as they walked to the front of the store and exited the building, with Morgan switching off the lights and locking the door behind them. "Where do you live? Do you want a ride? I wouldn't mind."

Morgan froze. "Oh, no. It's okay. I'm fine. I'm used to the bus." Jet could tell she seemed uncomfortable with the idea.

"It's really not a problem. I don't mind at all."

"No, thank you. See you tomorrow—up with the sun and all that!" Morgan trotted off toward the bus stop, quickly waving over her shoulder.

MORGAN

There was no way Morgan wanted Jet to see where she lived. It wasn't that her apartment was in a *bad* neighborhood, but it was a far cry from where most of those who frequented *Cold Brew* lived. It was in the old part of town, and the incomes certainly didn't match those of many in the area. It felt like it was always last on the list for upkeep and revitalization efforts, but Morgan had always thought it had its own unique charm with its beautiful architecture and history. She hoped someday the area would get the attention it needed to really shine.

As the bus pulled up to the stop, she glanced back toward *Cold Brew*, but Jet was gone. He had surprised her over the course of the day. She'd certainly learned not to judge a book by its cover—or a person by the first interaction. As she thought about Jet, her mind wandered to the encounter with his brother at the café earlier that morning. She reached a hand into her pocket and gripped the panties she had slipped there after he'd returned them, groaning. *How embarrassing!*

Climbing up the bus steps, she smiled at the driver and found a seat. She pulled out her book and began to read but struggled to focus again. Just as she closed her book, giving up, her phone vibrated with a text notification.

Jace: *Hey, pretty girl. You never answered my question. Do you want to grab some dinner?*

Morgan blushed. *He certainly isn't shy,* she thought. As she considered her still-empty refrigerator, dinner out didn't seem like a terrible idea. Still, she couldn't help but think about Jet's warning to keep her distance from Jace. Somehow, the draw of a good meal outweighed Jet's words of advice—and it was just one dinner. What could be the harm?

Morgan: *I'm in. Where should we meet?*

Jace: *Charmed to Table? It's the local farm-to-table, recently updated menu and whatnot. Supposed to be really good. I can pick you up if you want.*

Morgan laughed, realizing not only was *Charmed to Table* owned by her boss, but she'd also just returned from Main Street only to be considering going back there for dinner. *Oh well, I've been meaning to try it anyway.*

Morgan: *I'm in. See you in an hour and a half?*

Jace: *You got it. It's a date.*

With limited time to shower, Morgan threw her phone

aside and started tossing her barista clothes off as quickly as she could before stepping into the bathroom. Shortly after, she found herself, once again, staring blankly into a closet that had little to offer by way of date-appropriate apparel.

Why do I have no freaking clothes?! Morgan flipped through the hanging dresses, finally settling on a pair of black leggings with a gray, knee-length, short-sleeved sweater dress that flattered her curves. She paired it with short, black suede booties and a long silver necklace adorned with a feather pendant that hung down to mid-chest level. She examined herself in the mirror, added a touch of makeup and a coat of pink lip-gloss and thought, *Not bad for limited prep time!*

Morgan grabbed her purse, keys, and phone and headed back out the door to catch the bus back downtown.

Shark Cooter

MORGAN

Chapter 11

MORGAN EXITED the bus and began walking toward *Charmed to Table*. It was a relatively small downtown area, and she enjoyed the evening walk. The air had a crispness to it as fall bit at the heels of the summer heat. She had worried about being too warm in her sweater dress but assumed the restaurant might be chilly—and it wasn't like she had many options!

While most stores were closed for the day, their front displays offered charming window-shopping opportunities. Morgan enjoyed peeking into the different shops as she strolled toward the restaurant. When she arrived, right on time, she pulled up her phone and texted Jace.

Morgan: *I just got to Charmed. Are you here yet?*

Radio silence for a few minutes, but Morgan figured Jace

was probably still driving. Since this was Ben's restaurant, she headed inside for a drink at the bar. She assumed Ben, Gia, or both were probably in there. They found it hard to stay away. Since they'd been trying to get her to go in for dinner for months, she figured she might as well pop in for a bit to chat before Jace arrived.

Morgan entered the restaurant and greeted the hostess.

"Hi, table for how many?" the woman asked, smiling.

"Well, I'm waiting on someone. He's meeting me here, but I'd love to have a drink at the bar while I wait. Is Ben or Gia around? I work for them at *Cold Brew.*"

"Oh, you must be Morgan. They've mentioned you! Ben always said to take care of you—and that your meal would be on the house if you ever actually showed up. I assume that means you should order whatever you want from the bar, too. Ben's in the back sorting some supplies that just came in, but I'll tell him you're here." As Morgan walked toward the bar and pulled out a stool, the hostess pulled out her cell phone and started typing—likely a text message to Ben.

Morgan ordered herself a mojito. Within minutes, Ben appeared at the back of the restaurant and started walking toward the bar. "Ahh, Morgan herself. In the wild. Without a barista apron. I can't believe my eyes. Am I dreaming?!" Ben feigned blindness, rubbing his palms against his eyes.

"I do leave the house occasionally, you know."

"Sure, you do—to go to work." Ben poked her in the ribs. "So, who are we meeting?"

Just as Ben said those words, the front door opened, and Jace appeared. He walked up to the hostess, then saw Morgan out of the corner of his eye and began to wave.

"Ahh, there's my girl! I'm meeting her," he said to the hostess, gesturing to Morgan. "We'll take a table for two, as private as you can make it." He winked at her, and as soon as he began walking toward Morgan, the hostess rolled her eyes.

Morgan was slightly uncomfortable with the phrase 'my girl' being used on a first date, but she assumed he was just being friendly. She glanced toward her boss to see if he'd sensed anything strange about it, too. It only took a moment for her to register Ben's confusion at the sight of Jace.

"You and Jet are—"

Morgan interrupted Ben mid-sentence. "No, no. That's not Jet. It's Jace... It's his twin brother. They're twins." Morgan realized that, yet again, her words had come out a little less articulately than she'd planned. *This always seems to happen in Jace's presence.*

Ben looked Jace up and down, his eyes wide. "Remarkable." He shook his head back and forth as he took in the many similarities and subtle differences between Jet and Jace. "How do you and Morgan know each other? Through Jet?"

"No. It's kind of a long story," Morgan said, trying to prevent Jace from revealing anything that could lead to any depiction of the embarrassing laundromat underwear incident. She was sure it would be a funny anecdote someday— but not yet.

"Alright, one day you'll tell it to me." Ben chuckled. "In the meantime, take your drinks to the back room—through those doors. It's a party space, but it's empty tonight, so you may as well enjoy the quiet. Lord knows you need it after a day of slinging drinks at *Cold Brew*. Dinner and drinks are on Gia and I, so get whatever you want! I'll send waitstaff back there shortly."

Jace looked at Morgan and let out a slow whistle through his teeth. "Well, look at you getting the VIP treatment. I'll still owe you a date after this, since I'm not paying. Guess we'll have to do it again sometime." Jace winked at Morgan, lifted her drink to carry it for her, and followed Ben to the back, where he quickly set a table for two.

Jace pulled out the chair for Morgan, and she sat, appreciating the gentlemanly gesture. She couldn't help but think he was laying on the charm a little thick, though. Or maybe she just wasn't used to being treated right. Then again, she recalled her last relationship; they all started out nice at first.

Morgan admittedly had a lengthy history of making poor choices when it came to dating. The most recent one—she was engaged—led to her financial demise, which she was still recovering from, not to mention the loss of most of her possessions and a stint in a hospital to recover from a barrage of domestic violence-related injuries. The physical injuries had healed much faster than the mental ones, though.

Yeah, that didn't go well. I sure know how to pick 'em. A deep anxiety crept in as her mind wandered, but she took a swig of her mojito to silence it and began browsing the menu.

"Everything sounds delicious," Morgan said, eyeing the appetizers, then moving down the entrée list.

"It sure does," Jace agreed. "Wanna share this to start?" He pointed to the local charcuterie board option on the menu, holding it up for Morgan to see.

"Sure," Morgan said. "But you have to order it. I can never pronounce that word."

"That's fair," Jace said as the waitress approached their table.

"Hi there. I understand you are Ben and Gia's friends. I'm Amanda, and I'll be taking care of you this evening. Can I start you off with an appetizer, perhaps?"

Jace glanced at Morgan, grinning, then said, "Yes, thank you. We'll have the *shark cooter* board." He emphasized the two words, drawing intentional attention to the mispronunciation. Morgan winced and face-palmed herself, a slight chuckle. "What? Did I say *shark cooter* wrong?" Jace asked, feigning confusion. Morgan's giggle transformed into a cackle and, seeing Morgan's eruption, Jace and the waitress couldn't keep straight faces either. Soon, all three of them were crying from laughing so hard. Unable to get herself under control, the waitress held her hands up in a friendly 'that's enough' gesture and walked away to put the order in.

"Shark cooter!" Morgan declared. "Really?! Shark cooter?!"

"What? Is that not how it's pronounced?" Jace raised an eyebrow.

"No!" Morgan started laughing again.

"Then, how do you say it?"

"I already told you. I can't!"

"Then, it sounds to me like we'll be referring to it as 'shark cooter' from here on out, won't we?"

"I guess so!" Morgan agreed, sipping her drink.

"Then, cheers!" Jace said, raising his drink toward hers. "To shark cooters, mojitos, and first dates." Just as they clinked their glasses together, the curtains separating the private room from the restaurant opened.

There, standing in the doorway, was Jet—and he looked angry.

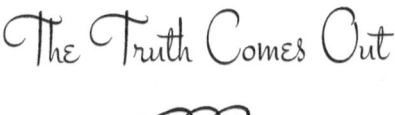

The Truth Comes Out

JET

JET'S ARMS were folded across his chest, and his expression could only be described as furious.

"Ben told me you were here, Jace. He was surprised I didn't tell him I have a twin brother in town," he began. "Now, why would I ever want to keep *you* a secret? Go figure." He scoffed. "Leave her alone. Turn off the charm. She's a good person. And, if she knew the type of person you are—I mean, who you *really* are—there's no way she'd be sitting across from you right now. I was going to let this go, and maybe it's still not my place, but I can't let you break her. You've destroyed enough lives already."

Jace glanced at Jet from where he still sat at the table and held his gaze, his eyes icy. Finally, he pushed up with both hands and slowly rose to his feet. "Well, if it isn't my little brother—again. You sure have a way of appearing at the least opportune moments, don't you?"

"I could say the same about you," Jet retorted. "Leave Morgan alone. Or should I reveal what caused the little rift in our fraternal relationship?"

Jace scowled. "Listen, bro—it takes two. That wasn't all on me. Your future wifey played her role... and she played it quite well, too, if I may say so myself."

"You could have walked away. You get a kick out of ruining people's lives. I won't let you do it again."

"Come on, bro. Wifey begged for it. You're a guy. You get it. Nothing I could have done. Just poor timing on your part for walking in when you did," Jace said, smirking.

Jet winced, remembering the excruciating moment when he opened the door to his bedroom and found his fiancé and twin brother in a very compromising position in his own bed. It was an image he couldn't cleanse from his mind, no matter how hard he tried. He had loved her deeply, and losing her, especially under such unfortunate circumstances, left a wound that would never truly heal. It was part of the reason he'd left town—to get away from her. Although he greatly regretted moving to the same area as Jace, he had to be where the band was. He'd hoped to be able to avoid him, but so far, that had been an epic failure.

"Morgan, may I introduce you to the *real* Jace—my fiancé-stealing, womanizing, cheating bastard twin brother. He can turn on the charm, but it's only a matter of time before the truth comes out. What are we on now? Two of my girlfriends and a fiancé?" Jet narrowed his eyes, glaring at Jace. "It's his M.O. He steals them, sleeps with them, gets bored, cheats on them, then leaves them crying. And that's just the beginning."

"Not my fault that *your* ladies like me better." Jace shrugged, clearly unbothered by the accusations.

"It's a game to you, Jace. And this round is over."

"Says you," Jace said, a smirk crossing his face. "Morgan, I'm sure, can see past these little transgressions. And, if not, there are plenty of other fish in the sea. Although, none with eyes quite so green."

Jace winked at Morgan, who had remained in her seat all this time, staring back and forth between the two brothers. Her eyes widened as she took in the scene before her, boggled by the audacity. Finally, she spoke.

"I don't know how I get into these situations, but it's getting old. Listen, Jet. Thank you for the warning and the inside information. I'm sorry you went through all that—and because of your *brother*, no less." Morgan forced a smile at Jet, appreciative of his protective gesture. "As for you, Jace, I've seen and heard all I need. This date is over. You can lose my number." Morgan rolled her eyes at the older twin, realizing the gentlemanly façade of their past interactions was nothing more than a well-rehearsed act in a role he'd played many times before.

Ben's voice boomed in from the back of the room. "... and don't show up at *Cold Brew*—or here—ever again. You're not welcome anywhere near my staff or at any of my businesses. Trust me, I have eyes everywhere, and it's well within my means to take the measures necessary to ensure that you keep your distance. Now, get out of my restaurant before I have the police forcibly remove you!"

"For what?"

"It's my business. I don't need a reason. And if I do, I'll come up with something—or I'll simply remove you myself."

Jace glanced at Ben and realized how serious he was. He raised two hands before him in a gesture of 'you win' and strutted toward the door, throwing a mocking wave over his shoulder.

MORGAN

Morgan's jaw dropped and hung there momentarily. She had never heard Ben so angry, let alone imagined him making threats. Warranted threats, but threats nonetheless. He was typically laid-back and easygoing, and getting a rise out of him took a lot. He must have overheard the confrontation between the two brothers. Morgan knew he was protective of her and his other staff members, looking out for them however he could. Ben and Gia felt more like her family than her employers most of the time, which was probably why she'd taken on so many extra shifts to help them. Well, that—and the money.

"Thanks, Ben," Morgan said. "I can handle this from here, though. It's not my first rodeo. I have a habit of going on dates with the wrong men."

"You tell me if he shows up again," Ben said. "In the meantime... Jet, sit. I said Morgan was getting a free dinner, and she is. And, since you're here, so are you. Sit." Ben gestured at Jet, ushering him toward the chair across from Morgan.

"I appreciate it, Ben, but you don't have to do that. I'm good. Really." Jet stood awkwardly near the table where Morgan still sat. He shifted his weight uncomfortably.

"I insist. You came all the way here to help another staff member, and for that, you get fed! It's the very least I can do. Morgan has carried *Cold Brew* with only Gia and me to help for quite a while now. We're glad to have you on board, and you've certainly proved that you fit in with our little family through your actions tonight."

Ben pulled the chair opposite Morgan further away from

the table and, again, indicated that Jet should have a seat. Jet shrugged, giving up the fight, and sat down as Ben handed him a menu. "All right, kiddos, I'm off! Promised I'd drop off dinner for Gia and her kids. Order whatever you want. Apps, dinner, drinks, whatever. Although, I don't suggest consuming *too* many drinks given that I know what time you both have work in the morning."

They groaned in unison. All three were all too aware of how soon morning shifts at a coffee shop came back around!

Crystal Returns

MORGAN

"THANKS FOR LOOKING OUT FOR ME," Morgan said after Ben had left the room. "I know you didn't necessarily want to tell me all that... but I appreciate it. I just wish you would have filled me in on some of those little details *before* I accepted the date."

"I did try to warn you. I just didn't really know what else to say without saying *everything*. There's a lot more to the whole thing, honestly. But, now I've told you what you need to know to make the right choice about Jace, at least." Jet's eyes housed a deep sadness Morgan could tell he was trying to conceal.

"Well, I appreciate it. We don't have to stay. I mean, you don't have to stay here with me if you don't want to. Ben will probably get annoyed if he finds out *I* left without eating anything, but *you* can go." Morgan did her best to appear nonchalant. She didn't really feel like eating alone, but the prospective awkwardness of sharing a meal with Jet—especially after what had just transpired—was daunting, too.

"No way," Jet started. "My brother stranded you here dinnerless. And I haven't eaten either. So, let's just... let's eat!" Jet's demeanor seemed calmer as he pulled out the chair across from Morgan and sat, picking up the menu. "Wow. Everything sounds incredible," he said, his eyes moving from the top of the menu to the bottom, then back up to repeat the pattern on the opposite side.

"I know. I was just saying that! I can't decide!" Morgan grinned across the table, feeling more relaxed as she sipped her drink. She took a deep breath, shaking off the lingering uncomfortableness.

"Hey, I have an idea. You open to something a little crazy?" Jet raised an eyebrow at Morgan, his lips curling up in a half smile.

"How crazy are we talking here?" Morgan asked.

"Not like... crazy, crazy... just a tiny bit crazy. Let's ask the waitress to surprise us!" Jet said. "Unless something jumps out at you that you really want—then we can order it, of course."

Morgan smiled, intrigued by the idea. "Actually, that sounds like fun—I'm in!" Morgan hadn't seen anything on the menu that she *didn't* want to try, so a surprise seemed just as good as picking out something herself!

"Sweet!" Jet said, waving the waitress over. "So... we are going to do something a little unusual, but then again, in case you hadn't noticed, the way this entire evening is unfolding is unusual, so we may as well continue the trend. Can you just... just..." Jet struggled to find the words to explain what they wanted to do.

"Just surprise us!" Morgan finished for him. "We'll take whatever you most recommend, or what Ben suggests if he's still here, or... whatever you have cooking already that's easy. Whatever! Just surprise us." The waitress looked momentarily uncertain but then shrugged.

"Entrees and apps?" she asked.

"Yes, please," Morgan said with a smile. "Ben probably wouldn't have it any other way."

"You're absolutely right." The waitress grinned at Morgan. "He already told me you weren't allowed to skimp. All right. A surprise it is." She nodded and left the room. Seconds later, Ben peered around the doorway from the kitchen area with a sly grin plastered across his face, then disappeared again. Both Morgan and Jet noticed the glint in his eye and looked at each other, eyebrows raised.

Simultaneously, they declared, "Uh oh."

"If Ben's involved in this order, it will be incredible but possibly a little exorbitant," Morgan told Jet. "He doesn't do things half-assed, so I hope you're hungry!"

"Oh, I'm a bottomless pit if the food is good!"

"Oh, it will be, just—potentially excessive. So, now that we've gotten our order out of the way, or lack thereof, dare I ask what you'll be doing about Crystal?"

"What do you mean what will I be doing about Crystal? Nothing. Why do I have to do anything about Cry—oh." As Jet glanced toward the doorway into the main dining area, following the path of Morgan's gaze, he saw the young woman sitting at a table with two female friends. They were situated in the perfect position to peer directly into the private dining area when the curtain was pulled open. As she caught Jet's eye, she gave a little wave and giggled to her friends.

"What is she *doing* here?" Jet mouthed, concerned.

"Well, under the circumstances and how this evening is unraveling, I would assume either a strange coincidence or that she followed you here somehow."

"Followed me? That's crazy!"

"Maybe—but not entirely impossible, either."

"You said she was harmless!"

"I thought she was... maybe she is." Morgan shrugged. "Maybe she's legitimately just here to eat." Morgan glanced into the main dining area again. As Ben walked by on his way out of the restaurant, he noticed the table of girls with their eyes trained on the inhabitants of the private dining room— his VIP guests. Pulling the curtain separating the two spaces closed, he strode toward Morgan and Jet.

"I really *am* trying to leave," Ben said, chuckling. "It's just one of those nights. Uh, I see Crystal is here... uh... spying? Sorry 'bout that. I'll make sure they keep the curtain closed. Food is on the way!"

"Yeah, we don't really know *what* she's doing," Jet said. "I guess. Maybe spying." He groaned.

Ben nodded. "Alrighty, so... curtains closed!"

"Please," Jet confirmed. "I have no idea what she wants from me."

Morgan grinned at Jet. "Oh, I have a pretty good sense of exactly what she wants from you. But, like I said, she's a little young."

"A little? A lot young, Morgan. She's *a lot* too young. She's not even *legal!*" Jet reiterated.

"... but in a few weeks," Morgan added, "she will be!"

Ben chuckled. "Let's just hope she gets bored quickly. Anyway, your food will be out in a minute. Hope you're hungry!"

"How hungry, exactly?" Morgan asked, glancing at Ben.

"Pretty damn hungry—and prepared to take home left-overs, too. Anyway, enjoy! I'm running out, so you're in my staff's capable hands—but they know to take care of you."

"Thank you, Ben. We appreciate it," Morgan said graciously.

"Yeah, thanks, Ben. Can't wait to see what you've planned for us!" Jet added.

Ben gave a slight bow, chuckled, and then walked back toward the curtain leading to the main dining room, pulling it closed behind him in a grand gesture. Neither Jet nor Morgan could miss Crystal—and her friends—craning their necks to get a view into the private dining area.

They didn't have time to think much about it, though. Moments later, several waitstaff members walked out of the kitchen and over to their table, each carrying a tray filled with platters, each overflowing with food.

"Your appetizers have arrived," their waitress told them.

"Appetizers? That's just *appetizers?*" Morgan asked, eyes wide.

"... yep!"

The waitstaff began piling plate after plate onto the table, pulling another over to add the overflow.

"You've gotta be kidding me," Jet said. "This is enough for ten people—or more!"

"Told you," Morgan said, grinning. "Ben doesn't do things half-assed."

It Isn't Real

JET

Chapter 14

MORGAN AND JET filled their plates with copious appetizers, entrees, and, finally, dessert. Ben's selections covered all the bases, from extraordinary salads featuring fresh produce from local farms to handcrafted ice cream made in-house with cream from the nearby dairy.

As they ate, the conversation flowed—as did their drinks. By the time the waitstaff brought the dessert platters out, Jet was relatively sure neither of them could even pretend to be sober. Laughter rang out as they joked about life as baristas and the differences between indie coffee shops and corporate. They shared both heartfelt and horror stories about their very different experiences.

"I can't eat another bite!" Morgan finally declared, holding her hand on her stomach for effect.

"I know. I'm stuffed. I don't remember the last time I ate so much!" Just as Jet was finishing his sentence, their waitress appeared with a pile of empty takeout containers.

"Ready to wrap up your leftovers?" she asked.

"Absolutely. Everything was amazing!" Morgan said, smiling.

"I'm glad you enjoyed it! It looks like you'll both get several more meals out of the remainder, too!" The waitress waved toward the back of the restaurant, and several kitchen staff members appeared. Working together, they quickly compiled the food into the containers and placed it into two large bags, evenly split.

Jet reached into his pocket and pulled out his wallet. He knew the meal was complimentary, but coming from the service industry, he would certainly be leaving a large tip for the incredibly helpful staff.

"Nope," the waitress said, eyeing Jet's wallet. "Ben said you'd probably try to tip. I'm supposed to tell you that he's handled it already. Very generously, I might add. But, we all appreciate it—thank you!"

Morgan chuckled. "Of course he has. I told you. Ben doesn't half-ass things."

"I guess not!" Jet said. "Alright, we ready to head out, then?"

"I think so," Morgan said, rising from her chair, grabbing one of the takeout bags, and passing it to Jet, then picking up the other for herself. As she started walking, she stumbled a bit, gripping the table for support.

"Alright, let's roll. As it turns out, I'm going to be taking a cab home, so if you'd like to share, feel free! My treat. Take a break from the bus. I can even get dropped off first if you're still uncomfortable with me knowing where you live."

"You could tell?" Morgan asked.

"Yep."

Morgan rubbed her chin thoughtfully, then finally agreed to share the car service. As Jet pulled the curtain to the main dining area open to walk out, his jaw dropped, and he quickly closed it again.

"Shit," he said.

"What?" Morgan asked. "What's wrong?"

"She's *still* here."

"No way!" Morgan exclaimed. "We've been here for hours! We ate a whole MENU's worth of food!"

"See for yourself," Jet said, gesturing to the main dining area.

Morgan peeked out through a tiny crack. "Doesn't she have a freaking curfew or something?"

Jet shrugged. "Guess not. Listen, I have an idea, but don't get mad at me."

"Why would I—"

Before Morgan could finish her sentence, Jet wrapped his arm around her waist and urged her toward the front door. "Let's go," he said, "if you're okay with this, that is."

Morgan immediately understood, and Jet assumed that, with how tipsy she probably felt, she wouldn't mind the extra support for walking, either. Two birds, one stone. It didn't occur to Jet to worry about the long-term implications of faking a date with his co-worker to get a fangirl off his back.

"Let's go!"

With Jet's arm around Morgan's waist, they emerged from the curtained area, looking like a couple. Crystal's eyes widened when she saw them, and a scowl formed across her pretty, young features. Morgan and Jet tried to walk toward the exit without any interaction, doing their best to ignore her, but as they passed Crystal's table, she called out to them.

"Morgan! Jet! Well, fancy meeting you two here! I've been meaning to try this restaurant for so long. Did you enjoy your meal? I didn't expect to see you two together outside of *Cold*

Brew, especially that you'd *just met* and all." Crystal enunciated the words "just met" for emphasis since Morgan had made that abundantly clear earlier in the day—and indicated she didn't know if he was single.

"What can I say?" Jet jumped in. "I guess we just really hit it off during the workday today. Isn't that right, Morgan?"

"Absolutely. We just... we just didn't want to part ways after our shift ended, I guess."

Crystal's eyes were like stone. "I see. And... you enjoyed yourselves?" she asked flatly.

"We did! Hope you had a lovely meal, too. Well, we'd better be on our way. Early morning shift and all," Jet said, an overly friendly smile plastered across his face.

Crystal nodded. "Yeah, sure. Bye," she muttered, clearly offended by their "date."

As Morgan and Jet turned to leave the restaurant, Morgan paused at a small alcove by the exit and glanced at Crystal and her friends, who were whispering amongst themselves. It was late, and they were no longer seating diners. The hostess had moved from her position at the entrance, making it relatively private but still within Crystal's line of vision.

"Kiss me," Morgan said.

"What?" Jet asked, staring at her with a confused expression.

"Kiss me. Make it look real. Just do it. She's more likely to leave you alone."

Jet shrugged, then nodded. "Okay, you want her to see real? Let's do real, then." With one hand still lingering on Morgan's waist, he placed the other on the back of her head, gently rotating her to face him. As he moved his face closer to hers, he gazed into her eyes and whispered, "You sure?" as his warm breath crossed her lips.

Jet intended it to be all for show, but as his eyes caught hers, he felt an overwhelming desire to hold and kiss her—for real. He blinked to curb the intensity of the moment, but it did little to stop his heart from pounding.

"I'm sure," Morgan said breathlessly.

"You asked for it," Jet whispered in her ear, his lips brushing against it as he placed his hands on both sides of her face and slowly moved it toward his. He tilted his head to the side slightly and met his lips to hers, running a hand through her hair, then onto the nape of her neck, which he held firmly but gently.

It isn't real, he reminded himself. *It's just to get fan girl to quit following me.*

The only problem was... it felt real. The whole thing felt real.

The Couch

~~~

MORGAN

Chapter 15

BEFORE MORGAN even knew it was happening, Jet's lips were pressed to hers, and she felt as if the world was spinning. As far as kisses were concerned, it was pretty tame. It's not like they were making out in the middle of the restaurant or anything. Still, it felt so full of passion that Morgan had to break from the kiss and take a step back to catch her breath.

She could have easily gotten caught up in it... but she knew she had to remember it wasn't real. *It isn't real.*

"Did she see?" Jet asked, bringing Morgan back to reality.

"What?" She blinked, confused momentarily.

"Crystal. Did she see us?"

"Oh, right." Morgan moved her head quickly back and forth a few times, shaking off the daze, then glanced toward the table where Crystal and her friends sat. She noted the downturned eyebrows and jutted-out lips of Crystal's pout. "Pretty sure she saw."

"Okay, good. Mission accomplished, then, right?"

"Right." Morgan's knees were weak, but she forced a smile, blaming the wobbliness on her alcohol intake. One kiss couldn't possibly make her so shaky—could it? She couldn't help but wonder if Jet had felt something too—something more than a fake kiss between co-workers. She changed the subject, attempting to erase such thoughts from her mind. "Did you order our ride yet?"

"I'll do it now. My treat, by the way," Jet said, pulling out his phone and opening the app. After hitting several buttons to ping their location to order a pickup, he added, "Let's wait outside. It's beautiful out."

Morgan nodded, glancing toward Crystal's table, then back at Jet. "Well, may as well finish this thing," she said, dropping her hand down and weaving her fingers through his as they exited *Charmed to Table*. As they stepped outside, the air was cooler than it had been when she arrived earlier. It was pleasant but somewhat sobering, and Morgan released Jet's hand, remembering it was all just a charade.

Jet smiled at Morgan as their hands separated. "Well, it's certainly been an interesting evening!"

"You can say that again," Morgan said, chuckling.

"Well, it's certainly been an interesting evening," Jet repeated, trying to keep his thinly veiled grin under wraps. Morgan rolled her eyes at Jet and began walking toward a nearby bench to await their car. Jet followed, sitting beside her.

"You sure you don't mind sharing a car?" Morgan asked.

"Of course not. I'd like the company. You sure you want me to get dropped off first? It's late. Are you going to be okay on your own?"

"I'm a big girl. I can take care of myself. I'm used to taking the bus and walking alone—this is nothing."

As the car pulled up to the curb to pick them up, Jet nodded his understanding. "Whatever you're comfortable with!" he said, opening the back door for Morgan and gesturing for her to go ahead. As she climbed in, the driver turned to face her. He was a big man, burly, with a long, unkempt beard and eyes that seemed to follow her every move.

"Hey there, little lady." His voice was scratchy and rough, like he'd smoked several thousand cigarettes too many. "Headed home? Seems like you've had a few drinks this evening. Care for some company? We could have a few more, you know?" The driver continued to speak, not realizing he was still awaiting the entrance of a second passenger.

"Uh, I—no," Morgan stuttered, looking uncomfortable. "Um... Jet?" she called.

Jet ducked his head into the car and followed it with the rest of his body. Glancing at the driver, he quickly realized the situation unfolding.

"No. My girlfriend is good, thanks," Jet said, narrowing his eyes at the driver, who scoffed at him. "And just the one stop is good—143 Webber Avenue," he added.

As the driver grumbled and turned to face the road, Jet glanced at Morgan, whose head was tilted sideways. She looked at him curiously. "Don't worry," he whispered. "We'll get you another ride home from there. I'm not letting you be alone with him in this car, let alone see where you live," he said. Morgan nodded silently, grateful that, twice in the same night, he'd been there to look out for her.

The rest of the relatively short drive was completed in awkward silence, thanks to the driver's repeated scowls and grumbles each time Morgan or Jet tried to drum up conversation between themselves. As they pulled up to Jet's apartment building, Jet ushered her out and then moved to walk beside her.

"Do you want to come inside to wait out the next ride?

I'm not sure how long it'll take since it's getting late and not as busy in this part of town as it is by *Charmed to Table*. Or I can hang outside with you. Whichever."

Morgan could tell that Jet was trying to make her as comfortable as possible, and at this point, she didn't see any reason not to trust him. "That works," she said, following him through a large door leading into his apartment building and up the stairs.

It was a nicer—much newer—building than hers. But as he led the way to his place and pulled the door open for her, she noticed how much smaller the apartment itself was. Jet followed her gaze as she glanced around the single space, furnished to contain a sleeping area, a small kitchen space with a breakfast bar for dining, a sitting area, and a bathroom.

It was kept neat for a bachelor pad, which she partially credited to him only recently moving in. The décor was limited apart from several hanging guitars, an amp here or there, and various musical equipment scattered around.

"It's just a studio," Jet shrugged. "Only me, after all.".

Morgan nodded. "It's nice," she said with a smile. She couldn't help but notice the way the apartment's lighting cast shadows across his face, giving him a tall, dark, and handsome vibe.

"It's okay. It works for the time being. I'm not here very often, honestly."

"I get that completely! Barista hours—especially when you've been the only barista—are brutal!"

"Yeah, that. And band stuff takes up a lot of my time, too. Come to think of it, I think you're the first person to see my apartment since I moved in. Have a seat. I'll see about getting you another ride home." Jet pulled out his cell phone and entered his location, waiting for the app to tell him the wait time.

He winced. "Uh oh," he said aloud.

"What's wrong?" Morgan asked.

"Uh... how would you feel about sleeping on the couch? Or I'll sleep on the couch, and you can have the bed."

"Why would I—" Jet held up his phone so Morgan could see the app. "Oh," she said. On the phone, an image indicating a wait time of 2+ hours met her gaze. She leaned her head back and stared at the ceiling. "Of course." She chuckled. "Of fucking course."

"I mean, we have to be up at the crack of dawn for work anyway. May as well just crash and go in together, no? You choose—the couch or the bed."

Morgan glanced at the bed in the corner of the room, then at the couch. Somehow, sleeping in her new co-worker's bed felt strange, even alone. She sighed. "The couch."

This night just keeps getting weirder and weirder.

Sleepover

JET

Chapter 16

JET COULD TELL Morgan wasn't thrilled about the prospect of spending the night at her trainee's apartment—but he really had been trying to protect her from the creepy car service guy! How was he to know that ride services were so scarce at this time of night? He had his own car!

He walked toward the bathroom and opened the closet, where he kept a few spare sheets and an extra blanket he'd used on his bed when it was still cool out. It was far from luxury bedding, but it was clean, and it'd keep Morgan warm enough. He dug through the bathroom drawer, trying to find an unopened toothbrush.

"I had one here from the dentist. I know it," he said aloud to himself.

"What?" Morgan called out from the sitting area.

"Nothing. Just getting you some overnight essentials."

"I'm fine. Really. It's only for a few hours at this point," Morgan said, glancing at her phone and noting the late hour. "Late" had a different meaning to baristas who habitually woke up before the sun to sling caffeinated drinks for hours on end. "I'm pretty low maintenance, and I have supplies at the café for the morning."

Jet nodded. "Still, you didn't ask for any of this. I'm sorry your evening worked out so... crappily," he said, laying a sheet out over the couch. He set up the blanket on top of the sheet and placed a pillow on one side. "And... Tada!" he said, pulling a toothbrush still in its package from behind his back and holding it up. "Brand new."

"Thank you," Morgan said. "And, for the record, my evening was far from crappy. Definitely unusual—but more interesting than any I've had in a very long time. All in all, it was pretty decent, actually. I enjoyed a great meal with good company and probably a few too many drinks—even got a goodnight kiss out of it," she joked, regretting the words the moment they escaped her lips and triggered an awkward silence.

Jet busied himself with smoothing out the blanket. After what felt like an eternity, Jet smiled. "It wasn't bad on my end either. I got to pretend to be on a date with a beautiful woman. Far from terrible, if I do say so myself."

Morgan's eyes flew open wide, and her voice caught in her throat. "You think I'm beautiful?" she mumbled, still unsure whether her head was spinning from his words or the booze. She let herself plop down on the couch, tired and a little dizzy.

Jet gazed at the ceiling, searching for the right words. Finally, he admitted, "Anyone who doesn't must be blind," while fiddling with the toothbrush package he still held. "That car guy certainly did, too!"

Morgan smiled and raised her eyes to look into Jet's. She examined his features, taking in his high cheekbones and full mouth. His dark brown eyes sparkled. "Wanna sit?" she asked quietly.

He shrugged. "We should probably just go to sleep. Early to rise and all'a that jazz," he said, trying not to offend Morgan with the subtle rejection but also not wanting to appear as if he was taking advantage. Over the past several minutes, he'd noticed that she seemed to succumb to the amount of alcohol she'd consumed a bit more. He knew that what she needed more than anything was to sleep it off. Morning would come all too soon—and coffee shops were unforgiving of hangovers!

Jet looked over and realized Morgan was sitting on the couch with her head held in her hands, and she didn't look well. "You okay?" he asked. Morgan looked as if she was trying to nod, but before she could make the entire head motion, she leaned forward and... *Ugh!*

"Oh, shit! Morgan, let's go. Come here." Jet reached an arm around Morgan's back and draped her arm over his shoulder for balance, silently thanking his lucky stars that he didn't have carpeting in his apartment. However, the couch would need a bit of cleanup. "Let me walk you to the bathroom." He guided Morgan, sitting her in front of the toilet, pulling her hair away from her face, and then tying it back more snugly.

Morgan turned to glance up at Jet. "I think I'm okay now. I think I just... the food. The drinks. I'm not used to it. Can I just go to bed now?" She groaned. "I'm so embarrassed."

"Don't be," said Jet. "It happens to the best of us. Musician, remember? I have a long history of digestive pyrotechnics in my repertoire." He held Morgan's hand as she stood, guiding her back to the main area of his apartment, past the couch and toward his bed. "But I thought—"

"I'll take the couch."

Morgan was too drunk and tired to argue, so she allowed herself to be put to bed and tucked in between the blankets. "Sleep it off. We've still got work in the morning," Jet reminded her as he turned away.

"Jet? Wait. Can you—uhm—can you stay with me? Please?"

Jet looked down at Morgan, who still looked worse for the wear. He was no stranger to feeling extra needy in the midst of a drunken escapade, so he sat on the side of the bed and smiled at Morgan. "Sure," he said, tucking a stray hair behind her ear. "Go to sleep, party animal. I'll stay here."

Morgan nodded, closed her eyes and turned onto her side, pulling the covers up to her neck and snuggling in for the night. Jet planned to wait until she was asleep, then relocate to the floor or the couch if he could clean it up well enough. He hoped most of the mess was contained on the blanket...

MORGAN

Morgan heard her phone alarm ringing incessantly. She brought her hands to her head and held it, massaging her temples. *Ouch. This workday is going to suck.* As she slowly regained consciousness, she became aware of a body beside her. Her eyes widened, and she froze. It took a few moments to remember where she was—and who she was with—and even then, everything was still foggy.

She slowly rotated. *Jet! Oh no. Did we? No way!*

Jet began to stir beside her before opening his eyes, also confused for a moment. He blinked a few times, then seemed to get his bearings. "I meant to move," he started. "After you fell asleep, I planned to move. I must have dozed off. I'm sorry."

Relief crossed Morgan's face, and she stretched her arms over her head. "So, we didn't... I mean... nothing happened, right?" She didn't think she'd forget if anything physical had transpired between them but figured she should double-check.

"Nope. After we got here, sleep. Just sleep. Well, after you christened my toilet with its first taste of digested food and mojitos."

"What?" Morgan looked confused. "How'd I wind up in your—oh!" All of a sudden, Morgan's face flushed a deep pink as she remembered the trip to the bathroom and the events that led up to it. "I'm so, so sorry! Is your couch okay?"

"No worries. It's okay. Really." Jet smiled at Morgan. "It happens. Get up. We need to get ready for work. That sounds weird—we. Anyway, uh, go ahead and shower in my bathroom if you want. Do you have black clothes at *Cold Brew*? I can try to see what I have here that could work. It won't be particularly feminine, mind you."

"I always keep a spare set at the café in case I manage to throw a vat of creamer on myself or something, and, before you ask, yes, I've done that on several occasions."

"Okay, cool. I don't think my black jeans and t-shirt would mesh well with your artsy chic style, but for the car ride there, I'll lay out a pair of sweatpants and a shirt in the bathroom. They'll be big, but that's what drawstrings are for." Jet grinned, tossing a clean towel toward Morgan.

"Thanks, Jet. Thanks again. For everything."

"Of course," Jet said. "That's what friends are for, right?"

Morgan grinned. "So, we're friends now?"

"I mean, I guess. I've saved your ass twice in the couple of days we've known each other. We've consumed a meal together, gotten drunk together, and had a sleepover. I think it's safe to say we're more than just co-workers now."

A shiver went down Morgan's spine at the words "more than co-workers," taking her by surprise. She knew Jet meant it platonically, but still, she couldn't get that kiss—and the comforting feeling of waking up next to Jet—off her mind.

Morgan made a quick recovery, rolling her eyes at Jet. "Listen, buddy, this is a two-way street. I saved your ass with Crystal, didn't I?!"

Paid Time Off

JET

Chapter 17

JET GOT ready quickly and cleaned up the mess from the night before as best he could while Morgan showered. He waited for her in the kitchen area while she threw on his "temporary clothes" until she could get her spare work outfit from her storage cubby at *Cold Brew*.

When Morgan emerged from the bathroom in Jet's sweatpants, which were several sizes too large, Jet couldn't help but notice how cute she looked. She had pulled her hair into two tight braids, which fell gracefully down either side of her head, giving her a sweet vibe that Jet found undeniably alluring. The sweatpants were closed with a drawstring that held them up somewhat, but even so, they sat further down on her hips than her own would have. The curved neckline of the tank top he had given her also fell lower on her more petite frame, leaving little of her cleavage to his imagination. The shirt, far too long, was tied in a knot over one hip, causing it to cling to her curves.

"What?" she asked innocently. "Do I look ridiculous? I look ridiculous."

"No, I just—it's good. I mean, it looks fine until we get to *Cold Brew*. Speaking of which, we'd better get going. All set?" Jet adjusted his own pants as discreetly as possible, trying to conceal the effect Morgan was unknowingly having on him.

Morgan nodded and grabbed her purse from near the door, where it had sat since the night before. As Jet ushered them out of the apartment, he suddenly stopped short, remembering that his vehicle was still sitting in the parking lot near *Charmed to Table!*

"Uh..." he started. "It occurs to me that we have two choices—attempt to get a car through the app again, or you teach me the bus routes in this town at record speed. My car. I totally forgot it isn't here."

"I did, too. Although, a good chunk of last night is still a little hazy, so that's not surprising. We can take the bus." Morgan looked around, gauging where they were while trying to picture the bus route in her mind. "There's a stop not too far from here—and I think we can catch one that'll get us there in time. Anyway, with the two of us, we can open really fast." She groaned and added, "Even hungover."

"Speak for yourself," Jet said. "I'm just fine, thank you. Unlike some people, I can handle my liquor." He glanced at Morgan sideways, a playful smile playing up the corners of his mouth. She rolled her eyes at him.

"Yeah, yeah, yeah," she said. "Okay, let's go. Before we miss the bus and really have a problem."

Jet and Morgan began walking toward the bus stop, which was only a few blocks from Jet's apartment. As they made their way, Jet consciously pushed back the powerful urge to intertwine his fingers with Morgan's and hold hands the way they had at the restaurant the night before. *It wasn't real,* he told himself, forcing his arms to remain at his side as they reached the bus stop and stood, waiting for their ride.

MORGAN

Did he just reach for my hand? No. I must be losing it. We don't have to pretend anymore. It wasn't real. ACT NORMAL, Morgan. Morgan took a deep breath and tried to look casual.

"You okay?" Jet asked, interrupting her thoughts.

"Oh—yeah, just hungover is all," she said. "I'll be okay after some coffee and ibuprofen."

"Well, I guess we work at the right place, then," he joked just as a bus pulled up to the curb. Morgan glanced up and read the illuminated numbers on the sign above the bus windshield.

"This is us!" she declared, stepping forward to climb into the vehicle. She smiled at the driver, and he nodded back at her.

"Different stop today, young lady?" he asked. He was merely making conversation, but Morgan felt awkward, especially given her apparel, her hungover state, and the events of the night before. It didn't help that Jet was boarding right behind her, and she'd just been picturing him holding her hand. So, she simply nodded. *Feels like a walk of shame, only I didn't even get more than a kiss last night!*

"Yep! Long story," she said as she moved past the driver toward a seat in the center of the bus. It was still quite early—barista hours—so it wasn't crowded yet. Only a few other people were on the bus, and it would likely remain that way for the duration of the ride. She took an aisle seat, triggering

Jet to take the one directly on the other side. For a few moments, uncomfortable silence stretched between them until Morgan pulled out her book and pretended to read. Her head was still pounding, but at least if she looked busy, she wouldn't have to make conversation.

As the bus pulled up to the first downtown stop, Morgan stood up and gestured to Jet to do the same. They exited the bus and quickly walked to *Cold Brew,* arriving almost perfectly on time to open for the early morning shift.

"Well," said Jet as Morgan went to unlock the door to the café. "All things considered, that could have worked out worse. I mean, we made it to work on time, and my car is now within walking distance. You still look a little worse for the wear, but we'll get some caffeine in you, and you'll be just fine—like you said."

Morgan stopped suddenly, glancing at the lock on the door with her eyes wide. "Oh my God... Jet. Did we lock the door to *Cold Brew* last night?"

"Yeah, definitely. Why?"

Morgan put her hands to either side of her eyes to shield the early morning sun and peered into the building through the window beside the door.

"Oh, thank God!" she said. "It's Ben. Why the hell is he here so early today?!" Morgan pulled the door open. "Ben! You almost gave me a heart attack. Why are you here at this ungodly hour?" Morgan glared at her boss, her hands on her hips.

"If you would have checked your cell phone, you'd have known you could have stayed in bed this morning—and you could have saved yourself, uh, both of you, the bus fare!" Ben's gaze shifted back and forth between Morgan and Jet with his eyebrows raised.

Morgan pulled her phone from her purse and glanced at the screen. "It's dead," she noted, pointing out the obvious.

Ben scoffed. "I came back to *Charmed* after it closed last night to drop off a few things. I saw Jet's car still parked there, so I figured you two had made it a late night. Gia and I were going to fill in for the first shift—possibly all day, depending on how you two felt!"

"Ben! I appreciate it, but you know I'd never miss a shift at the café because of an irresponsible decision. That's not me."

"I'm well aware, which is why I wasn't going to ask you. My voicemail told you explicitly *not* to come in—and as Jet's manager, you were supposed to relay the message to him... but here you both are. And on time, I might add. Impressive. Although, Morgan, your apparel could use a little tweaking." Ben eyed her baggy sweatpants and tank.

"So," Ben continued. "Good night?"

"Nothing happened," Jet jumped in, gesturing to him, then Morgan. "It's a long story."

"No need to explain!" Ben raised both hands with palms out in front of his body, indicating he didn't want to hear it. "I just hope you enjoyed the meal. Anything else is between the two of you. Now, both of you, get out of here. Get some sleep. Paid time off. Now. Go!" Morgan opened her mouth to protest, but Ben grabbed her shoulders gently and turned her around to face the door. "Shoo!" he said. "Go back to bed. Whether it's together or separately is none of my business," he smirked.

"We're not—" Jet started speaking, but Ben cut him off.

"Not my business. Go!" Ben waved them off dismissively toward the door. "Get out of here or... or..." He rubbed his chin thoughtfully. "Or you're both fired! See you tomorrow."

The Nap

JET

Chapter 18

MORGAN WANDERED out the door in a daze, looking somewhat lost, and Jet followed.

"Did our boss just tell us to go take a nap under the threat of terminating our employment?" he asked.

"He did," Morgan confirmed.

"Is that even legal?"

"I don't know. I mean, he's still paying us," she said, grinning despite her still-pounding head. "Let this be your first lesson on Ben and Gia... They are unusual employers. Amazing and incredible, for sure, but unusual just the same. Remember, Ben's rich. Rich people are allowed to be eccentric. This is how Ben does eccentric, I guess."

Jet didn't quite know what to say, but he decided to go with his gut and follow the confusing emotions that had been nagging at him all morning. *Might as well extend the weirdness for one more day.*

"Uh, hey, Morgan?" he said, his voice quiet with a slight tremble.

"Yeah?"

"Do you... Uh... would you like to take a nap with me?" he asked awkwardly. "Just sleep. I promise. Waking up together, it was... kind of nice, wasn't it?"

Morgan glanced at Jet quizzically. "Seriously? Are you really asking me to join you for a random morning nap?"

"I mean, only if you want." Jet began to feel uncomfortable with his decision. *What the hell is the matter with you, man?! You can't just ask a beautiful woman to take a nap with you!* He tried to ignore the overwhelming urge to face-palm himself.

Then, with surprisingly little hesitation and only a moment's thought, Morgan said, "You know what... I could use a good nap, actually."

"Really?" His face was a combination of shock, amusement, and relief.

"Really."

Jet laughed. "Okay, so, a purely innocent early morning nap amongst friends, it is! And, not that I didn't thoroughly enjoy our bus trip this morning, but let's take my car back this time."

With Morgan by his side, he turned to walk toward *Charmed to Table* to procure his vehicle and drive them back to his apartment.

MORGAN

What was I thinking? Agreeing to take a random nap with a man who is practically a stranger? Who does that?! I mean, not a stranger stranger. After all, we worked a shift, had a meal and some drinks, and I spent last night in his apartment. Oof, that sounds weird. Then again, this whole thing is WEIRD.

Morgan's mind was spinning, but this time, it wasn't from alcohol. She couldn't decide if she should back out or go through with it. *A nap? I mean, if it was just a nap, what was the harm? The whole thing was ridiculous!* But, at the same time, waking up next to Jet had been incredibly comforting. She couldn't help but say yes to a sober repeat—not to mention, his apartment was much closer to *Cold Brew* than hers, and she really wanted to close her eyes until her headache calmed down at least somewhat. *I hope he has a pretty hefty stash of ibuprofen.*

When they reached his car, Jet opened the passenger door for Morgan, then closed it behind her and got in on his side. He turned the key, triggering the stereo system to start playing *way* too loudly for someone with a nasty hangover—especially before 6 AM. Morgan winced and put her hands to her ears as Jet turned the dial down. "Wait," Morgan said. "Was that your band?"

"Yeah, I was listening to the few tracks we laid on our demo on my way to work yesterday to see how the recording came out. I'm sorry. I'll turn it off."

"No, don't. Just keep it a little low. I want to hear it."

Jet turned the volume up a little. "I'll put on the next track. It's a little less... heavy," he said, hitting a button on the console. The music was slow and deliberate, and the repetitive beat and smooth vocals felt like a lullaby to Morgan. She closed her eyes to take in the different harmonies that made up the song.

"This isn't you, is it?" she asked. "Singing, I mean."

"It is," Jet said. "Well, partly. The melody and lead guitar are. The rest of the band harmonizes on this track. This is one of our more experimental songs, and it's a lot calmer than most of the others—more melodic vocals. No yelling." He chuckled.

"It's beautiful." She meant it; it really was!

"Thanks. I wrote it, too." Jet smiled as he turned onto the arterial that led away from the busiest section of downtown toward his apartment. Morgan was quiet, and her eyes were closed, but she began silently mouthing the words of the chorus the next time it played through.

As the next song began, Jet attempted to turn it off. Even from the first two notes, it was obvious that it was a lot harder, louder, and more chaotic. Maybe not the best choice for someone with a throbbing headache, but Morgan stopped him from pushing the button. "Leave it. Just keep it low. I like it," she said, filling him with pride.

"It's like a dance between the characters. You can hear it in both the lyrics and the vocal tones—even the instruments. You get a sense of their emotion. The love, jealousy, rage, and so on. It's all there, duking it out to see which one reigns supreme."

JET

Morgan's words struck a chord with Jet. He couldn't remember the last time someone had truly listened to his music and "got it" the way she seemed to. That was precisely his goal when he'd written and recorded the song—and even his bandmates hadn't really understood the ultimate goal of the effort.

"Thanks," Jet mumbled.

He didn't know what else to say. His words were caught

somewhere deep inside, behind a wall. He thanked his lucky stars that they were pulling up to his apartment building—that is, until he thought about his lack of any solid plan for the next step. *How does one even begin to take a nap with someone they don't know? What was I thinking? Are there rules? What are they? Can we cuddle? Can I touch her if it stays innocent? What if it doesn't stay innocent?*

The thoughts came in torrents, but he did his best to shake them off and keep his cool as they walked up the very same stairs they'd stumbled up the night before. He opened the door for Morgan and followed her inside.

Fortunately, Jet's worries were unfounded. Without even a word, Morgan walked over to Jet's bed, climbed in, slid under the covers and curled up on her side with her head on his pillow. She gazed over at him, still standing by the door. "You coming?" she asked, sounding as if it was just a normal, everyday activity among friends, which, he supposed, it *could* be. *Why not? Maybe it should be.*

Jet smiled, calmed by her casual demeanor. He walked over, crawled into his bed and lay down on his back beside her beneath the covers. "Alarm?" he asked.

"No need," Morgan said. "Just sleep. Sleep until whenever." And both closed their eyes to sleep off the remaining effects of the night before.

Rise and Shine

MORGAN

Chapter 19

MORGAN STIRRED, and her eyes opened slowly. She inhaled, closing them once again as she filled her nose with the familiar smell and took it in deeply. It was rich and inviting—bold. She could pinpoint the brew immediately—Ben's Brazilian blend. As a welcome, he had probably given Jet the same coffee sampler he'd gifted her the day he'd taken over as the owner of *Cold Brew*. For a moment, she was disappointed she didn't get to awaken next to Jet, but the feeling was short-lived.

Morgan couldn't remember the last time someone had made her coffee while she was still asleep, let alone experienced the sensory magic of rising to the scent of a freshly brewed pot of high-quality dark Brazilian roast. It had been years since she'd enjoyed the simultaneously comforting and eye-opening rise-and-shine perfection of someone else preparing the morning caffeine—even if it was her second "wake-up" of the day. Something about waking up to freshly brewed coffee made her feel taken care of and protected, and those were feelings she now barely recognized.

Morgan yawned and stretched. She was pleased to find that her headache had dissipated almost entirely. She pushed the blanket downward and kicked her legs over the side of the bed, then stood and walked toward the kitchen area where the smell was wafting from.

"Good morning, Sunshine. Again," Morgan said with a teasing grin, seeing Jet standing before the coffee pot in cozy-looking flannel pants and a black ribbed tank top, pulling two mugs from the cabinet above. She couldn't help but notice how good his arms looked with his tattoos exposed. She wanted to get a better look but didn't want to get caught staring, so she looked away.

"Ahh! Morning? No, no, no, no. You, my friend, must be confused." Jet grinned at Morgan. "You see, you slept through the morning hours, long past early afternoon, and you are now experiencing what it's like to wake up sometime between late afternoon and early evening. Coffee?" Jet tapped the carafe from which he'd just poured coffee into a mug.

"What time *is* it?" Morgan asked, surprised she had been able to sleep so late.

"Around three."

"What?! PM?! No way!" She was shocked. "When did *you* get up?"

"Don't worry. It wasn't just you. I only woke up a bit ago myself. I figured you'd appreciate rising to the irresistible aroma of decent coffee!"

"It's Ben's Brazilian brew, right?" Morgan asked.

"Wow. Yeah. You're good!"

Morgan smiled. She could win at name-that-brew any day.

"For the record, that's not just *decent* coffee—it's the absolute *best* coffee," she clarified.

"Ahh, okay. That's fair. Grab a mug from that cabinet over your head. Milk and creamer are in the fridge, and sugar is on the counter."

"No need," Morgan said, reaching to open the cabinet above the coffee pot before pouring coffee into her mug. She sipped a tiny bit from the top of her cup to be sure it wasn't too hot. "It's perfect just like this. Why ruin it with all that other garbage?" She took a larger sip and relished the feeling of the hot coffee going down her throat, teasing her senses with notes of chocolate and caramel.

Jet sipped his own. "Ahh, good girl. A woman after my own heart. Black coffee is the way it's supposed to be drank. And it *is* a good brew. I'll give you that! I'd ask how you slept, but given the hour, I'd imagine it was pretty decently." He grinned.

Morgan nodded, somehow suddenly barely able to form words after that *good girl* comment caught her off guard. Finally, she managed, "I can't believe I slept so late. This is crazy for me."

"Same," agreed Jet. "It was nice, though."

Morgan could tell the awkwardness from earlier was creeping in, so she tried her best to change the subject. "Did Ben call or text?"

"He did. I told him you were still asleep. I told him I'd be happy to go in for the afternoon/evening shift, but he said no."

"You told him I was still asleep? So, he knows we *actually* spent the morning together?" She slapped herself in the forehead for effect. "What did he say? What does he think?"

"I mean, it was his comment that got me thinking about it in the first place, and I don't really think it's his place to care either way. So, he didn't care. He said to stay here, sleep it off, and come in tomorrow. He and Gia are fine there."

Morgan groaned. "I feel like a bad employee."

"He said you'd say that. I'm supposed to tell you to be quiet and drink the coffee—his words, not mine," Jet said, chuckling. "And that if you feel *really* bad about it, you can do extra inventory in the storage room when it's quiet during your shift tomorrow."

"Really? He said that? How does that man know me so well?"

"Ben just kind of gets people, I think. And he wants to make them happy and feel valued. I feel like he's one of the few people I've ever met who is actually content—and he wants to share that with as many other people as he can."

"You're right," Morgan agreed. "It's rare, don't you think?"

"What? Being content, or wanting to share it?"

"Either. Both, actually."

"Absolutely. I'd strive for both if I were that content."

"You're not?"

Jet shrugged. "Nah. It's been a rough few years, honestly. I don't remember the last time I felt truly happy with life as a whole. In fact, I don't know that I've ever been as happy as Ben and Gia seem."

"Yep. I get that. Not many have been." Morgan placed her mug on the counter and looked up at Jet. His eyes had a sadness to them that hadn't been there before. She assumed he'd gotten lost in his thoughts. Thoughts of the past, maybe of Jace, and of all that he'd had and lost. Before she even knew what she was doing, Morgan reached for his hand and placed it on her waist, then cupped his face with her hands and brought her lips to his.

He tastes like the best coffee on Earth.

Almost Lover

JET

JET PULLED AWAY, uncertain. Then, he gazed into Morgan's eyes for a moment before putting his hand under her chin and guiding her lips back to his mouth. It started as a slow, sweet kiss—one that was unexpected for both.

As they began to lose themselves in the kiss, Jet's hand, still resting on Morgan's waist, began to wander slowly downward, following the curvature of her hips and over her behind, giving it a slow squeeze with his strong hand. Morgan lifted on her toes, enjoying the feeling of his hands on her body.

Jet widened his lips, opening the kiss up to slip his tongue between Morgan's lips and deeper into her mouth. As their tongues danced, Morgan moved her fingers up Jet's arm, gripping his bicep and moaning as she felt the effects of him carrying all that musical equipment around. She traced his tattoos with her fingers, then broke the kiss to move her mouth down his neck and across his collarbone.

Jet lifted his head and moaned, triggered by her breath on his neck as her kissing and nibbling moved toward his ear. He moved his hand back up, bringing it beneath the bottom of Morgan's shirt and slipping it under the clasp of her bra, which he unfastened with a single motion. She raised her arms, and he removed both shirt and bra, tossing them aside.

"You're perfect," Jet said, taking in her petite frame and small but beautifully rounded breasts. He lowered his head down to take a nipple between his lips and sucked, teasing with his teeth. He released her from his mouth and looked upward into her eyes. "What do you want?" he asked. "Tell me."

"I don't know," Morgan managed to say breathlessly.

"Tell me what you want, Morgan," he repeated more firmly. Despite his predominantly easygoing nature, Jet knew exactly what most women liked. He was no stranger to the idea that dominance was attractive to many—and he was well-versed in using it. Nothing crazy, mind you, but with just a few words, he knew he could have Morgan dripping if she wasn't already.

"Come on, good girl. Tell me what you want," he switched gears, trying out praise to see if it was a good fit for Morgan. Bingo! He could feel her body go weak in the knees with those two little words—good girl. He repeated himself: "What do you want, my good girl?"

It was as if Morgan couldn't speak. She merely pointed to the bed while groping him with the other hand on top of his pants, gasping when she felt his size. Within seconds, Jet lifted her, placing one hand beneath her knees and his opposite elbow under her neck for support. He carried her to the bed and laid her gently down, kneeling beside her. "You sure this is what you want, princess?" he asked.

Morgan nodded, moving her hands to the waistline of his flannel pants and trying to pull them downward, indicating to him precisely what she wanted with no words at all.

Jet removed his lounge pants but left his boxer briefs on. He had other ideas. "I want to taste you. Can I taste you, beautiful?" he asked Morgan, crawling toward her to trace a finger from her lower lip and down her chin before resting his hand wide on her neck for effect. He wasn't into the whole choking thing, but he knew that hand positioning that drove women crazy. *Maybe it's a power thing.*

Morgan nodded, her hips rising as Jet tugged the drawstring, causing it to untie, then pulled the too-big sweatpants down over Morgan's legs. They came off easily, and she wore nothing underneath, having had no fresh panties to change into under Jet's clothes.

"Oh my God," Jet mumbled as he looked at Morgan, taking in the sight of her without any clothes on. "Morgan. Your eyes. Your smile. Your body." He groaned, suddenly overtaken with emotions he wasn't expecting. Then, he froze, a panic engulfing him.

"What's wrong with it?" Morgan asked.

"Nothing. It's perfect. It's just... it's all just fucking perfect." He looked her over again and groaned, but this time not from pleasure. "And you have to go. Now. I lost control. I'm sorry. I promised it would just be sleeping. I swear, I meant it. I'm sorry. You should go. You have to go now." Jet stood up quickly and grabbed the sweatpants from where they'd landed, tossing them toward Morgan. In his boxer briefs and tank top, he moved toward the kitchen to grab the shirt and bra he'd removed and handed them to her.

"I'll call you a car, okay? There should be plenty of rides available at this time of day," Jet said. "I'm sorry."

115

MORGAN

Morgan dressed silently, stunned. *What just happened?* she wondered. *Did I do something wrong?* She moved toward the door and grabbed her purse, then glanced behind her at Jet, who was sitting on the bed with his head in his hands. He looked miserable.

Part of her wanted to run away. She felt rejected. Embarrassed. Pathetic. But... looking at Jet sitting there, she knew there had to be more to this than met the eye. She turned back toward him and walked back, sitting beside him. She was still for a moment until she determined whether he would try kicking her out again—but he remained silent, looking down to avoid her gaze.

"What just happened?" Morgan asked. "What did I do?"

"Nothing," Jet said, looking as if he was doing all he could to keep his emotions from overcoming him. "It's not you. It's me."

"That's what they all say," Morgan joked. "Sorry, bad timing. But, if you could explain what that was all about, I'd really appreciate it." Jet looked up and tilted his head back, still avoiding eye contact.

"I haven't—you know—" Jet gestured at her, then at the bed, "since my fiancé. My former fiancé. Jace. I just... I don't know what happened. I froze."

"Do you still love her?" asked Morgan. "Is that the problem?"

"No. Not at all. I'm over that—but I can't get it out of my head, though. The images. My brother. Her. I'm all messed up. You're too good for me to get tangled up with like this right now. I'm just... I don't know. Not to mention the fact that you're technically my boss. Although, I admit I was willing to ignore that tiny detail since Ben didn't seem to mind. Morgan, I need you to know that this isn't about you.

It's about me. You're unexpectedly wonderful. And you deserve better than what I can offer right now."

"I'm sorry you had to go through that, Jet. I wish I'd never met Jace. And, realistically, I'm not ready for anything serious —or even anything not serious—either. I've got my own history. So, what if we just forget this whole thing and go back to being just friends and co-workers? Friends and co-workers who *don't* nap together. What do you say?"

"But the nap was so good!" groaned Jet, a slight smirk creeping up his face.

"Nope. Sorry, pal," Morgan said, trying to diffuse any remaining static from the situation—she had to work with him after all! "You rejected me once. No more nap buddy for you!"

Jet let out an obnoxiously massive sigh. "I'll have to find some way to survive solitary napping confinement. Somehow, some way, I'll make it. I do ask for your support during this trying time!"

Morgan rolled her eyes. "Glad to see we can joke about this so soon. Listen, we make pretty good friends. And, despite my initial reservations, I kind of like being your boss. It's a power trip. So, let's just forget this whole thing!"

"I'll show you a power trip," Jet winked suggestively.

"No, actually, you won't. That didn't go well for you last time, did it?" Morgan smirked. "Okay, call me a car. I'm leaving. This never happened. I was never here."

"Don't be stupid. Let me drive you. Surely where you live isn't a secret after all of this?"

"All of what?" Morgan asked, feigning confusion. "All of this that *never happened*? Okay, fine. I see your point. Drive me home, then."

The Ride Home

MORGAN

JET AND MORGAN walked downstairs and outside to Jet's car in silence. Morgan wasn't sure what to say after their conversation in his apartment, so she figured she'd remain quiet unless Jet had something to discuss. When they arrived at his car, Jet held the door for her. *Ever the gentleman,* she thought. *Except maybe in bed...* Despite how things had worked out, she couldn't help but wonder where that situation could have led if it had ended differently. He certainly seemed to know what he was doing, which, in her experience, was rarer than one might expect.

She shook her head quickly, trying to kick the dirt out of her mind. *Out of the gutter,* she told herself. But, as Jet walked around the front of the car to get in on his side, her eyes wandered up and down his body, taking in its muscular form

—less obviously ripped than his obnoxious brother's—but not bad at all. *Cut it out, Morgan. You're being ridiculous... And you really need to get laid, apparently.* She couldn't help but chuckle at herself.

She certainly hadn't meant to do it aloud.

"What could you possibly be laughing about right now after all of that?" Jet asked, starting the car and bringing her attention back to the situation at hand.

She feigned ignorance once again. "After all of what? I have no idea what you're talking about. I'm just getting in my *friend's* car for a ride home after an unexpected day off work."

Jet rolled his eyes. "Okay, okay. I get it. It never happened. Regardless, what are you laughing at?"

"Nothing. Never mind." Morgan said, reaching to fiddle with the radio to keep herself occupied. She turned it up slightly, keeping Jet's band's music just loud enough to act as background noise. "Just something in my head. I do that a lot. Working with me, you'll learn to ignore it after a while."

Morgan chuckled. It was true. She was known for talking to herself while going through the motions at work and even laughing at her internal monologues. Ben and Gia made fun of her for it all the time, but they got quite the kick out of it— and it helped her process her thoughts!

"You haven't told me where you live yet."

"Oh," Morgan started. "Right. Sorry. Head toward the older part of town. I'm over there." Everyone knew the "older part of town" was, essentially, a gentle way to reference the less affluent part—the other side of the tracks, if you will. Morgan was relieved when Jet said nothing, put the car into drive, and pulled onto the road.

JET

Jet could tell Morgan was embarrassed when she admitted she lived in "the old part of town." There was nothing wrong with it, as far as Jet was concerned, though. The architecture was magnificent. The history, fascinating. If he had found a suitable apartment over there, he gladly would have chosen that neighborhood over his current place. Not only was it more affordable, but the community had a much more artsy vibe. Overall, it was more his taste than where he lived.

As they drove, it was quiet except for the sound of Jet's band playing on the radio. After the bedroom incident, Jet was pretty sure it was best for them to take a break from chitchat. As they neared the area in which he assumed Morgan lived, he glanced over at her. She didn't seem to be paying much attention, lost in thought.

"Morgan?" he asked.

"Mmhmm?" she said, looking up and turning to face Jet.

"I'm going to need some direction here..."

"Oh, sorry! I didn't realize we were here already. Make a left onto Elm up ahead, then right onto Bridgeview, then a quick right. There's a lot of one-ways because the roads are so narrow over here. I'm the third building on the right."

Jet nodded. He was familiar with this part of town, as he'd done a few gigs in the smaller bars while he worked to gain traction with his band. He followed her directions, finally pulling up in front of her building. Morgan hopped out of the car as quickly as she could, more than ready to escape the awkward situation and get into her own space, Jet assumed. She thanked him for the ride through the car window and gave a quick wave as she walked toward the steps, jumping a couple at a time to get to the entrance.

Jet's eyes followed her the whole way. *That ass, though.* He would have had to stop himself from staring, except that before he could force his eyes away, she had disappeared into the building. Jet face-palmed himself once he knew she was inside. He pulled away and navigated the one-way side streets back to the main road, then toward his apartment.

When he arrived, he headed to the kitchen to pour another cup of coffee. Having left the insulated carafe on the warming plate on the coffee maker, it was still warm. He inhaled the smell of coffee, remembering Morgan standing there in his clothes only a short time ago, then glanced at his bed. *Well, Jethro, you sure messed that up, didn't you?* He took a long swig of coffee without adding any sugar or creamer. It really *was a* top-notch brew—and Jet wasn't easily impressed by coffee.

Having napped a good portion of the day, then consumed several cups of coffee in addition to the one he was working on now, Jet wasn't even remotely tired. He was, however, hungry. He pondered for a moment before remembering the massive amount of food he had tossed into the fridge when they'd gotten to his place the night before. *Score!*

Jet grabbed what he wanted, careful to save half for Morgan, then shoved a plate into the microwave to nuke it. He pulled out his phone to text her.

Jet: *I'll bring your leftover food to work tomorrow.*

He chuckled at himself. *I sure can't stay away long, can I?* Jet couldn't help but wonder whether he should have just brought the food to *Cold Brew* the next day without texting Morgan that night, but it was too late. "I'm a grown man acting like a schoolboy with a crush when I had every opportunity to take what I wanted earlier." He muttered under his breath, "Idiot," as he pulled the plate out just before the microwave dinged. He nibbled on the top of a jalapeno to see if it was hot enough, then nodded and carried the rest of the plate over to the breakfast bar.

As he pulled a stool out and sat, his phone vibrated once, indicating a text.

Morgan: *Thanks! If you're hungry, you can eat it tonight. No worries.*

Jet smiled as he responded:

Jet: *I'll have half. The rest is yours. See you tomorrow—too early.*

I mean, at least she gets the challenges of early morning wake-up calls. Most of the women he'd dated, including his ex-fiancé, were appalled at the hours he had to be at work—not to mention his band stuff, which often went on late into the night. His schedule definitely contributed to problems in the past. *Enough so that my ex had the free time to form a physical attachment with my twin brother,* he thought.

Morgan: *See you tomorrow.*

Short and sweet. I shouldn't have texted her in the first place. I'm pathetic. Jet groaned, continuing to eat his food. He flipped on the TV, hoping to mindlessly zone out into someone else's life for a while! Even though he was wide awake, bedtime would have to be at a reasonable hour, or he'd face exhaustion the next day. He figured he might as well just veg out until then—until his phone vibrated again.

Morgan: *Hey Jet?*

Jet: *Yeah?*

Morgan: *I enjoyed the nap. Just saying... and if you say, 'What nap?' I'm never speaking to you again.*

Jet: *I did, too.*

Morgan: *Good. See you tomorrow.*

Jet: *See you.*

"What the fuck was that?" he asked aloud, stretching his neck back and gazing up at the ceiling. Jet stared blankly at his phone as if it were an unknown, potentially dangerous foreign object.

We Meet Again

MORGAN

DESPITE SLEEPING for a good portion of the day, Morgan was still tired and hungover when she arrived home. She managed to crash and stay asleep through the night easily—that is, once she forced herself to forget the stupid text she'd let herself send to Jet. As she woke up to get ready for work, however, she couldn't take her mind off it. *I'm such a moron. I have to work with this man! So much forgetting that the whole thing had ever happened.*

She scoffed at herself as she dressed, selecting an outfit from the sea of black apparel swimming in her closet. She grabbed Jet's clothes off the bed, which she'd slept in the night before, and tossed them into the laundry hamper. Morgan figured it would be appropriate to wash the articles before returning them. Admittedly, it briefly crossed her mind to keep them—they were so comfy, and they held the faint scent of Jet's cologne from sleeping beside him the day before.

"You stoppit!" Morgan told herself as she boarded the bus downtown, looking forward to a bit of peace before arriving at *Cold Brew* for the morning rush. She was hoping to get lost in the pages of a book for a while and to forget about the strange few days she'd had—at least temporarily. Unfortunately, her sense of calm was short-lived.

After no more than one stop and several pages of reading, Morgan felt a formidable presence standing beside her. As she glanced up, her jaw dropped. It took a moment to process the face fully and make the distinction between the two brothers. But a sick feeling of recognition washed over her as she noted the hairstyle, broad frame, facial features, and athletic apparel.

Jace.

As she stared up at him with eyes wide, he grinned broadly. "Well, if it isn't my little laundromat princess. We meet again! I'm sorry we were so rudely interrupted during our date last night. My brother has a tendency to—"

"I'm not interested, Jace. I've heard about you and personally witnessed more than enough to know I don't want to be involved with you. What are you doing here, anyway? Since when have you taken this bus?" Morgan studied Jace's face carefully, trying to determine whether his words were lies or truth as he spoke.

"It seems I'm having a bit of car trouble," Jace started. "It's the funniest thing—just wouldn't start up this morning, and I had to get to the gym. And now, here we are on the same bus! Ironic, isn't it?" A smile stretched across his lips as he attempted to charm her.

But this time, Morgan didn't believe a word that came out of his mouth. She reached into her bag, trying to pull out her phone and send a discreet text to Jet. If she could get a message to him quickly, she could ask him to wait for her at the bus stop—at least as long as he was running on time. He would know how best to handle the situation from there.

Despite knowing that Jace supposedly lived nearby—hence their first meeting at the laundromat—something about his presence on her bus left her feeling extremely uneasy. Until then, she hadn't really been concerned about him, but this felt close to a stalker-level coincidence.

Morgan felt around her bag, finally grasping her phone and pulling it out. *I need to clean this bag out!* She began typing as Jace slid into the seat across the aisle from her, leaning to peer over her shoulder. It was a violation of her personal space and privacy—what else was he capable of violating?

"Texting Jet? Oh, no, no," he said. "Don't text *him*. He ruined our time together last night. We don't need him to do it again, now do we?" Jace's voice had lost its charm, replaced by an almost menacing tone.

"Jace, I told you. I'm not interested." Morgan searched her mind for an escape. "In fact, I, uh, after you left the restaurant... I'm... We... uh... Well, Jet and I are seeing each other now." The final words gushed out quickly in a torrent. Morgan hadn't been able to think of anything else to say that would get him to leave her alone, possibly. *Oh no,* she thought. Maybe it would make things worse. He did steal his fiancé, after all...

Jet won't be mad, will he? Morgan asked herself. *I mean, I did the same thing for him with Crystal, right?*

"Well, I'm certainly sorry to hear that. You know, it wouldn't be the first time someone saw my... merit... over my brother's, though." Jace winked. "I'm more than happy to give you a test drive, baby. Then you can take your pick."

Suddenly, Morgan felt triggered, and she found her voice again. "Baby? Oh, no. I'm *not* your baby! That's awful! You're despicable! How could you think it's okay to take a woman from your own brother? And more than once? You have a problem, Jace. I'd never date you, knowing even just a portion of what I do now. Back off. Jet and I are happy together, and we don't need you creeping around!"

A look of pure surprise washed over Jace's expression. He looked as if he'd seen a ghost. Morgan imagined that not many women had ever spoken to him in such a way, blinded by his good looks and charm, then dumped before they had the chance. She stood up and skirted past him to sit in the seat directly behind the bus driver, who, fortunately, she knew well enough to ask that he keep an eye on her. She was certain Jace saw her whisper something in the driver's ear before sitting— and, if he hadn't, her words were given away by the driver's face as he turned to scowl directly at him. *At least I know people are looking out for me around here.*

Then, Morgan texted Jet, filling him in on the morning's events—all of them, including the new "fake dating" scenario she'd gotten them into. After what felt like an eternity, the bus pulled up to her stop downtown. She thanked the bus driver for his extra attention and climbed down the bus steps, seeing Jet waiting at the curb.

"Is he still on the bus?" he asked, an angry expression on his face.

"Yes," Morgan said, nodding toward the middle section of the bus where Jace remained.

"Good," Jet said. "And, sorry in advance for this..."

"For wha—"

Before Morgan finished her sentence, Jet's arms wrapped around her waist, and his lips were firm against hers. Jet's kiss was slow, deep, and passionate. Whether or not it was an act didn't matter one bit to Morgan at that moment.

Either way, her world was spinning.

JET

Again. Jace is trying to do it to me again! Jet read Morgan's first message over. From what he understood from her obviously rushed texts, Jace was on the same bus, hitting on Morgan after all that had happened the night before. *How did he know she'd be on that bus?* Jet wondered. While he and Morgan weren't *actually* together, he'd been firm that Jace was to stay away, as had Ben. This was a straight-up ballsy move, even from Jace.

And it was unacceptable. Jet began to consider the fact that perhaps Jace wasn't simply out to hurt him—but that he may be a danger to others, too—potentially physically.

As he continued reading Morgan's texts, he tilted his head back and rolled his eyes. "Oh Lord," he began. "Well, if she wants us to be a temporary couple again, I guess I owe it to her now. As if things weren't going to be awkward enough today, let's add one more random make-out session to the mix!"

Jet chuckled to himself, but as soon as he saw Morgan's anxious expression as she climbed off the bus, he knew what he had to do. He wanted to hold her. To comfort her. Their chemistry was undeniable, and, at that moment, he wanted nothing more than to let his brother see it firsthand—no matter how awkward things may be for him and Morgan later. A taste of Jace's own medicine, if you will—even if it was practically nothing compared to what Jet endured.

So, as soon as she reached the curb, Jet pulled Morgan toward him, placing his lips firmly but tenderly against hers. He held the back of her head with one hand while resting the other on her hip. He poured every ounce of passion he had into that kiss. From the moment their lips met, it was pure fireworks.

With several kisses between them already under their belts, they were no longer unfamiliar with each other's style and movements. Their lips moved against each other, tongues circling as if dancing. The deep, almost overpowering connection sent shivers down Jet's spine. His resting hand shifted to caress Morgan's back as the other moved to her face.

He kept her chin in his hand as he moved his mouth away and whispered, "They're gone," into Morgan's ear.

"Are they?" she asked, dazed. "Wait, what? Who?"

"Jace. The bus."

"Oh, right. Okay. Good. I... Uh... Thank you?" Morgan's words were jumbled as she shook off the power Jet's kiss held over her.

He grinned at her, letting go of her face and taking a step back, putting a space between them. "You're welcome. Now, time to get to work!"

Morgan glanced at her watch. "I guess it is, isn't it?" The two of them walked the rest of the way to *Cold Brew,* then proceeded through the morning opening routine, each acting as if nothing had happened between them. Externally, they were merely co-workers arriving at work and getting on with the routines of the day.

Inside, though, Jet was a mess—again!

Secrets, Secrets

JET

Chapter 23

Focus, Jet. Focus. He was struggling to accomplish even the most basic tasks at work, and it was driving him crazy! Morgan hadn't mentioned it, but he knew he certainly wasn't impressing her the way he had on his first day. Jet would have already fired himself if he were his boss!

In a matter of only a few hours, he'd managed to spill a latte all over himself, Morgan, and the counter. Fortunately, none managed to get on the customer. He had miscounted change twice, dropped a tray of baked goods while carrying it to the display, and burned himself on the steam wand more than once. He was, by definition, a total mess.

His mind just kept wandering back to Morgan—and not Morgan as his boss or coworker, either. He couldn't stop thinking of her in his sweatpants and tank top, lying in *his* bed next to *him*. He was trying not to admit the other visions that kept dancing through his mind, even to himself, but they were assuredly *not* nearly as PG-13. The heat in their kiss that morning wasn't helping the situation.

It was making him crazy!

As the day dragged on, Jet managed to get himself under control somewhat by avoiding thoughts of Morgan as much as possible, which meant avoiding *her*. It was no easy task, given their proximity to one another in the small café. By the time afternoon rolled around, he had managed to complete several customers' orders in a row without screwing anything up... Things were looking up until Morgan reached under him to access the baked goods while he was taking an order. She rubbed, he believed unintentionally, against the front of his pants, then glanced up at him with her eyes wide in surprise.

Oh, for the love of all things Holy, he thought. *She couldn't have felt that. Did she feel that?* He brushed it off, turned away, and adjusted his pants, which were, admittedly, tighter than usual around the frontal region.

"Sorry," Morgan mumbled as she grabbed the pastry for her customer and carried it to the counter where he was waiting, glancing back at Jet over her shoulder to gauge whether *he* knew that *she* knew.

As soon as their eyes met, both shifted their gaze immediately in the opposite direction. Yep. They both knew.

MORGAN

Well, he's definitely interested in me in one way, at least, unless that, uh, excitement, had been about someone else. Morgan pondered as she glanced around the café, trying to determine who could have had such an effect on Jet if not her. Most of the café's clientele at that time consisted of men and women escaping their downtown offices for an afternoon caffeine break. Most were significantly older. And there was a group of male construction workers who'd stopped in for cold drinks after their workday at the project site nearby. While she didn't *think* he swung that way, more power to him if he did.

As her eyes continued to search the room, they settled on the back area of the coffee shop, where Jet had come from just before he'd returned to the counter and taken the last order—just before the *baked goods incident*. Morgan narrowed her gaze in on the thin brunette surrounded by her high-school-aged friends: Crystal. *I didn't even see her come in.*

As the younger girl caught Morgan in her line of vision, she scowled. *If looks could kill,* thought Morgan. *Probably mad I'm "dating" her newest prospect, at least as far as she knows.*

Still, Crystal was a regular customer. She and the crew she traveled with brought a significant amount of business to *Cold Brew,* so it was essential to maintain a good rapport with them despite the stalker vibes Crystal gave off when it came to Jet. *Must be something in the water,* she thought, thinking about her earlier encounter with Jace on the bus.

"Hi, all! Didn't see you come in," Morgan said, addressing the entire group with the most cheer she could muster, a smile plastered across her face.

A few "Hey, Morgan's," "Hi's," and "Hello's" came pouring back—but Crystal remained silent.

"Let me know if you need anything!" Morgan said, offering a quick wave as she turned to head back to the front counter.

"Hey, Morgan..." Crystal finally spoke, addressing her directly.

"Yes, Crystal?" Morgan turned to face the younger woman, gazing quizzically at her.

"I learned the most *interesting* thing this morning before school—on a public bus, in fact. Don't *you* take the bus?" She peered at Morgan with icy eyes.

"I do."

"How interesting. And did you know that our new friend Jet has a *twin brother?* The resemblance is uncanny; only Jace, his brother, is even cuter. We had a lovely little chat. I bet you'd be *quite* interested in some of the things he had to say, given your new relationship with his brother and all." Crystal's voice came off in a forced saccharine-sweet tone—one that oozed with false pretenses.

Morgan stared at Crystal, shocked not only that she knew of Jace's existence but that they'd clearly had at least one pretty substantial conversation already, if not more. "Whatever Jace told you, I can pretty much guarantee it isn't true or that he manipulated it in some way to serve *his* purpose, whatever it is. Trust me, he's not a good guy."

"I'll bet Jet told you that, didn't he?" Crystal asked, waving her hand dismissively. "Jace said you'd say something like that. He said a *lot* of things, actually. And I'm sure he'll say a lot more when I meet him tonight."

"Crystal, he's way too old for you. And he doesn't have good intentions, I promise you. Listen. We've known each other for a long time. I wouldn't try to get in the way of something good for you."

"Oh, but you've already gotten in the way, Morgan. Telling me you didn't know if Jet was single just so that you could secretly go out on a date that very night." Crystal frowned, her eyebrows tilted down in anger. "Not nice. Pretty humiliating for me, don't you think?"

"That's not what happ—"

"Save it, Morgan. I don't need Jet. I'll have the better

brother soon enough. That's a fact. Trust me, though... you'll want to know the things I do. But now's not the time. Now, run along and get back to work. Your new employee seems to be having a rough go of things today, doesn't he?"

"How did you—"

"I have my ways." Crystal smirked at Morgan. "Plus, you're both covered in coffee..."

Morgan took a few steps back, moving away from Crystal and her friends, before turning and walking to the front of the store. When she got to the counter, she glanced over at Jet, who was standing in front of the espresso machine preparing some sort of latte and chit-chatting with one of their regular customers. The moment he saw Morgan, his expression became serious. He finished making the drink quickly, gave it to the customer, and pulled her aside.

"You look like you've seen a ghost! What's up? Is everything okay?" Jet asked, looking directly into her eyes.

"I—well—maybe. Or maybe you, maybe *we*... might have a problem. I don't really know what's going on, but Crystal and Jace are up to something." Morgan shrugged, still uncertain as to what the two had even discussed or why it could possibly matter to her.

"Crystal *and* Jace? Like, the two of them? Together? They know each other?"

"Maybe. She made it seem that way. I'm not entirely sure."

Jet glanced toward the back of the café, hoping to catch a glimpse of Crystal to assess her intentions—but she and her friends were gone.

"What the? Are they allowed to use the back door?" Jet asked, certain both he and Morgan couldn't have missed them leaving the café through the front door, despite being distracted.

"No, but they clearly did, anyway. I guess we'll have to start arming that back alarm even during the day... What a

pain in the ass! We use that door constantly for the dumpster."
Morgan scoffed.

Jet nodded. "This... could get messy."

"Why?" Morgan asked.

"It's complicated."

The Wounds That Don't Heal

JET

TRIGGER WARNING: REFERENCES TO SUICIDE ATTEMPTS.

COMPLICATED IS one word for it. Jet worked the remainder of the day taking orders, making drinks, and handling the day-to-day routine with Morgan at the café—but he was distracted. Both of them were.

Now, Jet couldn't stop thinking about Crystal and Jace. Sure, he had secrets, but was Jace so awful that he'd destroy his life *again* in a brand-new town? The short answer was yes, and he knew it. Still lost in his thoughts, Jace spoke aloud softly under his breath without even realizing it. "I knew I shouldn't have moved to the same town as him—band or no band!"

"Did you say something?" Morgan asked, glancing sideways at him.

"Oh, no. Sorry, I was just thinking aloud, I guess."

"Think aloud a bit louder next time, please, so I can actually help." Morgan smiled at him. He gazed at her face a little longer than he probably should have, taking in the green in her eyes and the way her tied-back hair fell over one shoulder. "What?" she asked. "You're staring."

"Nothing. I... It's nothing. Nevermind."

"You're being weird. We promised we wouldn't be weird." Morgan gave him a playful nudge to the ribs with her elbow. "So, act normal!"

"I know. I'm sorry. It's not that. It's—" Jet's words trailed off. He didn't know how to begin to tell her the *other* reason he'd left town. The real reason. Yes, his heart had been broken. His brother had betrayed him. But it went beyond the disaster between his former fiancé and his brother. *Way* beyond what he was willing to tell Morgan—or anyone for that matter, but Jace knew. Maybe Crystal did now, too.

After slinging coffee for several more hours, trying his best to avoid anything deeper than surface conversations with Morgan, it was finally time to close. Morgan mopped the floor, and Jet couldn't help but notice how cute she looked from behind as she moved the mop back and forth across the floor, still sticky from the combination of spilled coffee and sugar.

"What are you staring at... again!?" she demanded, taking Jet by surprise.

"Uh, you missed a spot," Jet said, quickly coming up with what he thought was an acceptable excuse.

"Pardon me?" Morgan held the mop out in the direction

of Jet. "Would *you* like to finish up, then?" she asked as she leaned against the counter and took a sip of the iced cappuccino that she'd been trying to finish for a good part of the afternoon.

"Fine. I was staring at your ass," he mumbled under his breath, giving up the fight.

Morgan started to cough, caught off guard by his brazen honesty. The last sip of coffee she'd taken went down the wrong pipe, and she began to sputter. Finally getting herself under control enough to respond, she slapped him on the shoulder. "Well, stop it!" she managed.

"You really want me to?" he asked, a note of flirtation in his voice.

She scoffed. "Since you've virtually ignored me all afternoon, and we haven't discussed the *many* elephants in the... café... yes! Yes, I do!"

"Which elephants are those exactly?" Jace glanced at Morgan, his eyes questioning.

"Where should I start? You and me, Crystal and Jace, and whatever it is that you're too scared to bring up from back home—because it seems like a little more than the broken engagement that brought you here at this point... not to minimize the trauma of that in any way."

Jet winced, realizing she wasn't just going to let this go, at least not long-term. She knew there was something more going on, and at some point, he'd have to fess up on the details if they were going even to stay friends—let alone more. If more was even an option, given that Jet had no idea how she even felt about him.

He took a deep breath and prepared to reveal his deep, dark secret.

"Okay, you want to know why I'm here—besides what I've already told you?" he began. "The real reason? Alright. Here it is... Yes, my fiancé Fiona slept with my twin brother, and yes, it crushed me. Completely destroyed me, in fact. I became a shell of a person—to the point where I no longer wanted to exist. The feelings of pain and betrayal ate at me until I couldn't function anymore. I stopped eating, started drinking *way* too much, and pretty much never left my apartment."

Morgan took a step toward Jet and placed a hand on her arm, but he shook it off. "I'm sorry, it's okay. You don't have to—" she started.

"No, I do. I want to. In fact, I think I *have* to tell *someone,* and I want it to be you. Anyway, finally, I gave in to the dark thoughts and decided to just let go. I didn't want to be alive, so I chose to end my life. Only, it didn't work, obviously. The details aren't important—but the *only* reason I am here is because my best friend Nate saved me and, in the process, lost his own life. He drowned. The guilt was inescapable at home. He rescued me and died for it. He was a hero through and through and successful in every single part of his life. Meanwhile, a man who didn't want to be alive is still here, floundering through life, playing in unknown bands and working in coffee shops. Worthless."

Jet leaned against the wall and let himself fall to the floor behind the counter, curling his legs upward and burying his face in his hands. Morgan lowered herself to sit beside him, placing her hand on his knee. "I'm so sorry, Jet. That's a lot. That's too much for one person!" Morgan squeezed his leg in a gesture of support.

"Nate was a golden boy. He was full of life and promise. He was going to be a doctor. And I couldn't face the fact that he was gone because of me. I couldn't look at anyone in town, especially Nate's family—who were more a family to me than my own—without sobbing. Everyone thought I fell off that bridge, and even despite their pain, they told me it wasn't my fault again and again. But they didn't know the truth—only

Jace did. He had even egged me on in a way, taunting me with what he had done with Fiona, telling me I wasn't worth anything to anyone, not even her. He told me I should end it all. And, at the time, I guess I felt like he was right."

"Jesus Christ, Jet. He's evil. That's literally evil."

"And you wonder why I'm concerned about him and Crystal..." Jet gazed at the ceiling, tilting his head back and blinking back tears.

"So, you just left?" Morgan asked. "You didn't tell anyone the truth, the whole story?"

"Pretty much. The town was already crushed. They didn't need any more sadness. They didn't need to know it was a tragedy that didn't even need to happen. You wanna know what's sad?" Jet asked. Morgan nodded silently in response but kept her eyes locked on his.

"Sure."

"Fiona obviously wasn't innocent in the sequence of events, but, in a way, she was also collateral damage in connection with something that should have only involved Jace and me. I knew what my brother was capable of, to a certain extent. Even then, I didn't think he'd go so far with *her*, knowing that we were supposed to get married. I should have protected her from him from the start. I didn't know."

The tears that had been welling up behind Jet's eyes over the last several minutes began pouring down his face as he tried to pull himself up, rising from the floor to escape Morgan's penetrating gaze as she sat dully, seemingly unable to find any words appropriate to the situation. She looked as lost as he felt.

Finally, the words came.

"Jet, this isn't your fault. It's Jace's. It's life's fault. It was a horrible tragedy, but you didn't mean to cause your friend any harm. You were broken. And, the truth of the matter is, we've all been broken in one way or another. Your case may be extreme, but we're all just working through the wounds life has inflicted, just trying to heal and do better. We all have scars from battles most people who pass through our lives know nothing about."

As she spoke, she flipped her wrist over, sliding the bracelets she almost always wore upward to reveal the nasty-looking scar that traveled vertically from her lower wrist to about a quarter of the way up her forearm.

How had I missed that the other night?

As if reading his thoughts, Morgan responded, "Makeup. I usually cover it."

Nothing "Putt" Friends

MORGAN

Chapter 25

JET AND MORGAN sat together on the floor of *Cold Brew*, and both of them let the tears flow. He had shared his story, and it was Morgan's turn. Hers wasn't as dramatically tragic—no one had died *except her, almost*. Just the same, there was solidarity in the idea that both had given up hope, thrown in the towel on life—and both were prepared to let the lights go out forever.

Both had tried.

Instead, they were forced to survive against their will, to start over from nothing and, from the ground up, build lives they could at least tolerate. They were forced to push through the days that came after.

"So, he left and took everything?" Jet asked, seeking clarification on Morgan's story. "No goodbye? No explanation? Nothing, just gone?"

I shrugged. "Uh-huh. While I was in the hospital after the last time he beat me up, he cleaned out the bank accounts, took everything from our old apartment and sold it—even my clothes. He didn't tell me he hadn't paid the rent in months. He just left me for dead, then disappeared. After I got out, I couldn't catch back up, and things kind of fell apart for a while."

Morgan traced the cut on her wrist with her pinky finger without realizing it. "I guess after all that I just didn't see the point of living. Time and again, the men who were supposed to love me and take care of me wound up hurting me—physically and mentally. I guess I just didn't want to give anyone the chance to do it again. And, life didn't really seem worth living anymore. I had nothing left."

"I'm so sorry," Jet said, squeezing Morgan closer. "Did they ever track him down? The last guy, I mean."

"Not yet. But I figure he's long gone at this point. He didn't really have any ties to this area beyond me, so... I don't think he'd risk getting caught by returning."

"That must have been so difficult for you," Jet said. "No closure. No answers. No justice."

Morgan looked thoughtful. It *had* been difficult, but in hindsight, it was the best thing that could have happened to her. Well, his leaving had been, anyway. She certainly could have done without the cuts, bruises, and hospital stint, but her ex had been toxic through and through. Over several years, he'd alienated her from friends and family, shredded her confidence, destroyed her ability to think for herself, transformed her into an anxious mess, and made her feel like she wasn't good enough for anyone else. Then, when there was nothing more he could do to hurt her mentally, he resorted to physical violence.

When he left, it took a while—and she was still working on it—but she was far better off. Slowly, she was becoming the person she had been before she met him... before he tore her down.

"Now that I've worked through some of it, I realize how many different ways he was hurting me. It's a unique situation from yours, I know, but it was traumatic," Morgan said. "My biggest fear is that he will do this to someone else."

Jet squeezed his arms around her tightly and intertwined the fingers of his hands. "Of course, it was traumatic. It's horrible. You deserve so much better. You should be taken care of and protected, not knocked down emotionally and damaged physically. That's not a man."

Sitting on the floor of *Cold Brew*, Morgan couldn't help but notice how safe she felt despite sharing with Jet things she'd never told anyone else in her life. She had never felt so vulnerable yet secure. *Talk about protected,* she thought, glancing down at his strong arms.

"Thank you," Morgan said quietly, turning to look at Jet. Suddenly, she felt trapped by his eyes. Like her own, they were red and puffy from crying, but somehow, it made tiny flecks of color—green and yellow, mostly—stand out against the brown, giving them an unexpected sparkle. As she felt herself hypnotized by them, Jet rested his cheek against hers, then placed a hand on her opposite cheek and turned her face toward his until their lips met.

The kiss was gentle and sweet. They held it for several seconds, lost in the calm after the storm of emotion they'd let out. Sitting, lips connected, wrapped in Jet's arms, there was comfort. There were no requests or indications of wanting to go any further. Just the kiss was enough. Morgan felt at peace.

As she and Jet pulled apart, he stood, reaching a hand down to help Morgan up. She could tell he didn't necessarily want to stop but was concerned about where it would lead—a valid worry given their recent bedroom interactions. She rose, using his hand to pull herself up.

"That was—uhm—" Morgan stammered, searching for the right words.

"Nice?" Jet finished for her.

"Yeah. Nice," she agreed. "I mean, the kiss part, the rest before that was, uh... tough."

"Tough but somehow cleansing, no?" Jet asked.

"Definitely."

"Okay, so," Jet started, "now that we know each others' back stories, can we finish closing this place up and get home?"

"Your home or mine?" Morgan asked, joking.

Jet rolled his eyes. "Don't tempt me. After kissing you, my willpower is *not* particularly strong. Fortunately for both of us —well, maybe... maybe not—I have a band gig. It's just at a small dive bar, but it's something. I mean, it pays, at least." Jet looked pensive as he finished his sentence. "Hey, you wouldn't want to come with me by any chance, would you?"

"As a friend and coworker?" Morgan asked, a slight smile making its way to the corners of her lips.

"As my manager, obviously. No, just kidding. As my date."

"Your fake date?"

"I think we both know that whole fake dating thing is getting a little old. I mean, what would make it seem more realistic to everyone we're trying to fool than to try *actually* dating? I think of it this way: you know that I've basically killed a man, and you're still sitting here with me. I take that as a good sign!"

Morgan rolled her eyes at Jet. "That's not funny. You realize that, right?"

"No, but I've learned that if I can't laugh at the fucked up shit in this world, I'll never make it out alive."

"But none of us make it out alive," Morgan pointed out.

"For the love of coffee, Morgan, do you want to go on a date with me or not?"

"Yes, I do. But I wouldn't be me if I didn't give you a hard time about it first. Now, mop that floor while I toss the garbage, then I'll try to make myself look less like a swamp monster. We rendezvous back behind this counter in fifteen minutes to get the hell out of this place!" A smirk took over as she added, "And, unlike *some* people who work in this establishment—and I'm not naming names—*I* won't stare at your butt while you mop."

Jet grinned back at Morgan as he grabbed the mop and started sweeping it back and forth across the floor. She turned to walk away, and he called after her, "Oh, come on! You know you want to look. Just a little peak!"

"I'm good!" she shouted.

"You don't know what you're missing," Jet said as he mopped, lifting the back of his shirt to put his assets on full display. He swayed his hips back and forth and wiggled his butt at her in a cute little dance.

"I said I'm good," Morgan reiterated, but she couldn't help herself. She turned and glanced back at Jet, then burst into laughter at the sight of his butt dance. She quickly pulled out her phone, hit record, and took a video. "Oh, Jet. Jethro, Jethro, Jethro. You're right. That *was* worth it. And I'm sure I'll find a way to use this video at some point in our... friendship... or whatever."

As she slipped her phone back into her pocket, Jet grinned. "You wouldn't dare," he said.

"Oh, wouldn't I? Garbage time!" Morgan called as she trotted out toward the back door to toss the bags into the dumpster.

An Unexpected Encounter

JET

Chapter 26

JET FINISHED MOPPING the space behind the counter before completing the remaining closing tasks inside the café. He was trying to conceal his excitement over the idea that Morgan had agreed to see his band play. As he thought about her, though, he realized he hadn't heard a peep since she'd left through the back door some time ago. *Did she come back inside to get ready without saying anything?* Her coming in without making any smart-alec comments or remarks about his mopping job was unlike her, but maybe she was nervous about the date or something.

"Morgan?" he called toward the back of the store where both the back door and restrooms were located. No answer. *That's weird.*

149

He walked toward the rear of the café and stuck his head out the back door, which was slightly ajar. There, standing in front of the dumpster, were three shadowy figures. As his eyes adjusted to the change in light, he could tell that two were women. He knew one was Morgan, as she was still holding the garbage bag she'd carried outside several minutes ago. It didn't appear as if she was being "held" there against her will in any physical way. Still, she looked nervous about moving from her spot in front of the dumpster, and her eyes were wide like those of a deer in the headlights.

Jet squinted to get a better look at the others—*Crystal and Jace,* he realized quickly.

"What are you doing here, Jace?" Jet's voice boomed with a deepness he rarely used—except occasionally when he was singing some of his heavier songs. Morgan's eyes widened a little at the unexpected tone.

"Ah, good. We've been expecting you. Just wanted to have a little chat, is all. Wanted to tell your new girlfriend a little bit about our history," Jace said, winking at Jet.

"You're several minutes too late, bro. I already told her everything. The actual truth, not your version—whatever you were planning to make it out to be."

"Oh, Jethro... You say *my* version as if I've made something up. We both know Nate didn't just *fall* off that bridge. The way I see it, he jumped after someone else who went down with self-destructive, uh, motives—or he was pushed. Neither of those stories fares well for your reputation around our little hometown, my brother. Regardless of what you've told your new girl, I'm sure Nate's parents and our little Fiona would love to hear *my* version of the way things went down—for perspective. Don't you agree?"

"Jace, leave me alone. This has gone on long enough, hasn't it? Don't hurt them by bringing this up in town. Let them have their closure—and let me have my life."

Beneath the single light illuminating *Cold Brew's* back parking lot, Jace's eyes were narrowed, lips pursed, and his brows were arched down in anger. His expression looked downright menacing. "I don't think it has gone on long enough, actually. You see, you two embarrassed me and Ms. Crystal—my girlfriend. And I don't think that's a very kind way to treat your regular customers."

Morgan and Jet let out a simultaneous groan at the word 'girlfriend' just as a car pulled into the lot, causing Jace and Crystal to nervously take a step away from Morgan. It freed up enough space between them for Jet to move past, standing before her in a protective stance.

The car pulled up to the dumpsters, causing Jace to jump out of its way, leaving Crystal in its path. The car came to an abrupt stop before it reached her, and Ben stepped out of the vehicle, glaring at Jace and Crystal.

"Ben," Morgan began. "How'd you know we were—"

Ben gestured up toward the light above them. "New camera," he said. "Felt like maybe this place needed some extra security back here. Noticed the back door was getting a bit more... traffic than usual yesterday. People snooping around." He enunciated the word 'traffic' as he glanced at Crystal. She looked down and shrugged as he continued. "I turned it on for the first time tonight while I was still down the street at *Charmed to Table.* Imagine my surprise to find two of my staff members and two of their... friends... congregating in my back parking lot. Figured I'd stop over and join the party." Ben smirked at Jace and Crystal, knowing they were up to no good. "Although, it looks like things are just wrapping up. Am I right?"

Ben stared first at Jace, then turned toward Crystal, waiting for a response. "Am I?" he repeated more firmly.

"Yes, Ben. The party is over. We're sorry," Crystal mumbled under her breath, pulling on Jace's arm to move him up the driveway that wrapped behind *Cold Brew* and toward the front of the building.

"Good. I'm glad we agree," Ben said. "And as for you..." He glanced at Jace and narrowed his eyes. "I thought I said I didn't want you anywhere near my staff *or* on my property. Was I in any way unclear about that?"

Jace rolled his eyes and, without a word, marched off behind Crystal toward Main Street, sulking.

After watching the two of them walk to the end of the block, Ben turned to face Jet.

"Ben, I—" Jet started.

Ben held up his hands. "Nope. I don't even want to know the details. You two should get out of here, though. Go home. Get some sleep."

"Jet has a gig," Morgan said. "He can't miss it."

Ben turned to look at Morgan. "Are you going, too?"

"I mean, I was. That was the original plan, but..."

"Okay, climb in," Ben gestured to the fancy car. "We'll all go. I'd love to hear our new barista's musical side. I went to your art gallery thing, didn't I? Run inside, grab your stuff, lock up, then get in the car. Leave anything that's not critical for the morning. "

Morgan smiled. Gia and Ben were the first to arrive at the show and the last to leave when several of her paintings were accepted into a local gallery exhibition. Then, without saying a word to her, Ben secretly purchased the paintings from the gallery owner and hung them in *Cold Brew* as a surprise. She'd been angry with him, as she would have *given* them to him, but he said she deserved the money.

"We finished almost everything up before. I just want to change my clothes," Morgan said, glancing down at her coffee-stained shirt.

Jet smiled. "You do that. I'll lock up."

"Alright, then, the plan's set. Get a move on!" Ben waved Morgan and Jet back into *Cold Brew*. "I'll meet you at the front door."

Tight Spaces

MORGAN

Chapter 27

MORGAN STOOD, peering at herself in the mirror, certain that fear was still evident in her eyes. She blinked it back, trying to get in the right frame of mind for an evening out—again. She sure was getting out more lately, at least! The way Crystal and Jace had cornered her by the dumpster while she was alone felt nothing short of terrifying. She took a deep breath to try to calm down. Still unsure of their intent, she thanked the universe for sending the guys to her rescue.

Quite frankly, I'm STILL sick of having to be rescued, she thought, scoffing as she pulled a folded midi dress out from her small storage cubby and tried to fit it over her head. Rushing to get ready to head out the door so Jet wouldn't be late for his gig, she somehow managed to get her arm caught in the head hole. As she maneuvered herself to adjust the dress, it threw her center of gravity off just enough to send her wobbling to the left, causing her to lose her balance.

Morgan reached out, grasping for the counter beside her to steady herself, but it was too late. She missed. As her feet slipped out from beneath her, she gazed heavenward, knowing that falling was inevitable. So, putting her physical well-being into the hands of the universe, she let it happen and braced for impact. Morgan felt her legs pull out from beneath, her body moving toward the floor as if in slow motion. On her way down, her arm grazed the massive stack of perfectly piled toilet paper rolls waiting to be stocked in the storage room.

She'd told Jet to stock them in that spot until they could better organize the storage space. It was a mess. *I should have done that earlier today.* As her flailing limb collided with the pile, rolls of toilet paper fell everywhere. From the floor, Morgan gazed around the room, momentarily stunned and unsure of what to do next. Her butt hurt, but that seemed to be the extent of bodily damage. So, there she sat on the floor, half-dressed, surrounded by toilet paper. *Classy,* she thought.

"Are you okay in there?" Morgan heard Jet's voice and started to panic. *How embarrassing!*

Suddenly, Jet's head came into view, peeking around the doorway. His eyes widened as he took in the scene before him, finding Morgan flailed out on the floor with toilet paper rolls covering the entire lower part of her body.

First, his jaw dropped, but when he saw that she seemed uninjured—beyond her pride—a smile climbed the edges of his face, and he started laughing. "How did you... how did you even...?" His voice trailed off as his eyes caught and lingered on her still half-on dress.

"Don't ask," Morgan responded. "I was rushing..."

Jet reached a hand down toward Morgan, but before she could grab it, he pulled it away. "Wait. One sec," he said, pulling his phone out and taking a snapshot of Morgan amidst the mountain of toilet paper. He returned his phone in his back pocket.

"What are you doing?" Morgan asked, narrowing her glare.

"Revenge and/or blackmail photo," he answered, wiggling his butt to remind her of the video she'd taken of him taken earlier. "I might need this later."

Morgan muttered something under her breath as Jet held his hand back out toward her. She grabbed it, pulling herself to her feet, then glanced around at the disaster area the room had become just as Ben walked around the corner, his eyes widening in surprise as he took in the sight before him.

"We can we just... Can we just fix this later?" Morgan was in the middle of asking Jet.

Jet chuckled. "You're the boss," he said. "Not my call."

"Yep," Ben jumped in. This definitely looks like a problem tomorrow. Let's get out of this place. Honestly, I could use a beer at this point... and I don't really even drink." Ben put a hand against his forehead in a facepalm.

"Fair enough," Jet said, "Let's roll, then!" He gestured to the toilet paper strewn about. "Get it? Roll?"

Ben grinned, rolled his eyes, and waved a hand dismissively. "I'll be in the car. Try to avoid any further disasters, huh?" Morgan and Jet nodded.

Morgan tried to conceal the smile threatening to emerge at Jet's attempt at humor. She also couldn't help but notice Jet's eyes wandering down toward her half-concealed stomach, her dress having not made it all the way over it.

"Maybe you should finish what you started there?" he said, indicating her half-on outfit. Morgan blushed.

"Nothing you haven't seen before," she purred, managing an exaggerated wink in a half-hearted attempt at flirting.

Jet grinned, shaking his head at the absurdity of the situation. "Indeed," he said, chuckling. "Get dressed. I'll meet you in the car," he told her, adjusting himself as he walked out the doorway toward the front of the store.

Jet

That woman is something else. If I survive this job with her around, it'll be a miracle! Jet walked out the front of the shop to where Ben had pulled his car up to the curb. It was a fancy, fast-looking sports car with all the bells and whistles. For the most part, Ben didn't act like he had money. Jet assumed this was his exception. It certainly wasn't a cheap vehicle!

"Climb in!" Ben beckoned through the open window. "It's gonna be a little tight, but you're riding shotgun. Morgan gets the jump seat—she's the smallest." Ben pointed to the single, small seat behind them.

"Good thing my bandmates have my gear in their van," Jet said, taking in the tight quarters.

As the men sat waiting in the car, Morgan appeared at the café door, turning around to lock it behind her before walking over to the car. Jet tried to avoid checking her out, but it was inevitable. The dress she'd half-worn just a few minutes earlier now hung perfectly over her curves, belted at the waist to accentuate her figure and give it an hourglass appearance. *Oof,* Ben thought.

She peered inside. Ben chuckled. She'd been in his car before, but she had always been in front, either getting a ride home from work or accompanying him on a work-related errand. She squinted at the tiny seat between the two men, set slightly back.

"You've got to be kidding me," she started. That's about big enough for a seven-year-old!"

"Accurate," Ben said. "Would you prefer one of us to try squeezing back there?" His eyes twinkled playfully as if he knew full well that she would come along with little to no fight. They all needed to blow off a little steam.

Morgan eyed the seat. "Fine. Get out a minute," she said to Jet. "I may be smaller, but I'm not *that* small!" Jet nodded, climbed out, then folded his seat forward, allowing her to squeeze behind it and into the tiny space she'd been relegated to.

"This had better be a good show," Morgan mumbled beneath her breath.

"Always is," Jet said confidently, grinning at her.

Musical Interlude

~∞~

MORGAN

WHEN THEY ARRIVED at *Dirty Martini,* the group fought their way through a sizeable crowd to get to the bar for a round of drinks. Being around large groups of congregating people fell pretty far down on Morgan's list of things she deemed enjoyable, but the bar service was prompt, and Morgan soon held a light beer. Keeping it simple.

As Jet headed to the back room of the bar to meet up with his bandmates, she and Ben headed to a less crowded area of the space that offered a good view of the stage area. Luckily, they snagged a table just as a couple stood up to leave.

"So," Ben began, "what's up with you two?"

"What are you talking about?" Morgan asked, feigning ignorance.

Ben rolled his eyes. "Morgan. This may come as a shock to

you, but I'm not an idiot. From day one, you and Jet have been doing *something,* and until now, I've kept out of it... but I'm curious, and we've always been close. So, I'll ask again: what's up with you two?" A playful smile tugged at the corners of Ben's mouth.

Morgan knew he meant well and was just looking out for her, but after the events of the evening thus far, she just wanted to sit back, drink her beer, and enjoy some music.

"Ben, I—"

Morgan hadn't had a chance to finish her sentence when the band members began strutting onto the stage from a room just beside it. When Morgan saw Jet, her eyebrows raised. *Wow.* He looked so different in his gig clothes. His band persona was similar to his ordinary, everyday vibe—but somehow magnified. He wore leather pants—tight leather pants—and a snug-fitting tank top. Of course, he held his guitar. Maureen's gaze locked onto his tattooed arms. *Oof.* She tried to keep herself from staring, but it was a lost cause.

Ben let out a cheer as the band took the stage, reeling Morgan's attention back. He was grinning at her. *Was I drooling? Am I that obvious?* He looked at her and shook his head, chuckling. "Absolutely nothing going on, right?" he asked.

Morgan rolled her eyes in his direction, then buried her face in her hands. "I have no idea," she admitted. "Just watch the show," Morgan pleaded, gesturing toward the stage, trying to escape the conversation temporarily, at least.

JET

Look at her. She looks so hot. Immediately upon moving onto the stage, Jet's eyes had searched the crowd for Morgan and Ben. When they honed in on them, he was pleased to see they'd found a table near the stage. For some reason, he was nervous. He used to get this way before gigs—ages ago—but now, he was pretty much a veteran when it came to playing in front of a crowd.

Somehow, Morgan's presence made it feel like an electrical current was running through his body straight through to his fingertips. He had been so impressed by how quickly she seemed to "get" his music that playing it for her live—the way it was meant to be experienced—felt like kind of a big deal. He glanced at the drummer situated behind and slightly to the left of him and nodded, indicating he was ready to begin the set. His drummer gave a countdown of four drumstick claps, and Jet dove in, playing the opening guitar chords to the first song. As the rest of the band joined in, music took over the space, enveloping the small bar in sound.

As he played and sang the lyrics to the same song that he and Morgan had listened to in the car together, he kept his eyes glued on her.

Everything changed without a moment's grace.
You emerged like a butterfly from some secret place,
Changed my world, lifted me high,
You became the star in my always starless sky.
Left me behind to spread my wings alone,
Soul torn asunder, heart turned to stone.

Jet strummed the guitar, feeling alive for the first time in what felt like ages. His words seemed more powerful than they had before—as if someone else was listening and actually hearing them. He kept his eyes on Morgan's expression, taking in each nod of her head, the way she closed her eyes during the chorus and the way she looked as if she *felt* the music somewhere deep inside.

Despite being distracted by Morgan's presence, Jet felt like his performance was boosted. By the time their intermission began, he was pumped! He felt like each song had been better than the last, and both Morgan and Ben seemed to really be feeling it. It wasn't that he needed anyone's approval, but it certainly felt good to have "friends" in his life again—even if it was confusing as fuck with Morgan, and both she and Ben were technically his bosses.

When they finished the last song of the set, the band moved offstage and into the room behind for a quick meeting. A few minutes later, Jet emerged and made a beeline for Ben and Morgan. As soon as they saw him, they began to applaud.

"That was amazing, man!" Ben started, slapping Jet on the back playfully. "I better be prepared to lose you to a world tour, I guess!"

Jet rolled his eyes. "I hardly think that'll become an issue, but thanks, Ben. I appreciate it."

Morgan smiled at Jet, adding her compliments. "It really sounded incredible," she said. "Way better live than recorded. Do you have time to sit before the next set?"

Jet nodded, pulling a stool out from beneath the high table and sitting with them. A few moments later, the three other guys who'd been onstage with Jet walked from the bar toward the table, slapping Jet on the back upon their arrival.

"Hey, Jet, you gonna introduce us to your friends?" one of the men asked, gripping Jet's shoulder.

"Oh, Marco, hey. Hey guys. This is Ben, my boss. And, Morgan, my—uh, also my boss, I guess," Jet stammered, struggling for the right words to describe their relationship or lack thereof.

Ben shook hands with the guys and offered his congratulations on the awesome first set. Morgan sat back and smiled, offering a quick wave and hello. It was impossible not to notice that Marco's stare had fallen directly on her, and Jet noticed her shifting uncomfortably in her seat. Jet eyed Marco for a moment, then wrapped an arm around Morgan's waist, hoping it would trigger him to back off.

"Oooh," Marco said, smirking. "THAT Morgan."

"Oh... Has Jet mentioned me?" Morgan asked, suddenly interested in the conversation. Marco and the other guys glanced at Ben, a snicker making its way through the group.

"Maybe once or twice," Marco said, smirking at Jet.

Jet coughed. "Oh, look," he interrupted the discussion, "it's time to get back to the stage for the second set!"

"How convenient," Morgan said, chuckling.

"Indeed," agreed Jet.

I Quit

MORGAN

THE REST of the gig went similarly to the first half—great music, and the crowd was really into it. Jet's extraordinary charisma stole the show as far as Morgan was concerned. She heard other females around her gushing about his hotness and felt a pang of jealousy. *What right do I have to be jealous? We aren't even dating. Not really, anyway.*

Fortunately, Ben kept any additional questions about her and him to a minimum—not that she had any answers to offer, anyway. It wasn't until the final song that anything unusual transpired.

As Ben sang the final few verses, he suddenly seemed to get distracted. His eyes shifted away from Morgan, where they'd rested for the bulk of the evening, and toward the door. Then, his expression changed, growing darker, and Morgan could tell something was off. Jet's eyes narrowed as his gaze trailed from the entrance across the room as if following something, finally settling at the bar area. As the final notes of the song rang out, Jet looked uneasy as he nodded his head toward the bar, peering directly at Ben, trying to signal him to look that way.

Ben craned his neck, sensing his meaning, and turned toward the front of the building. There at the bar sat Crystal and Jace. His arm was wrapped around her waist possessively. Morgan's eyes widened as she noted their presence at around the exact same moment. There was no way their appearance was coincidental.

"What are they doing here?" she hissed at Ben.

"I don't know, but I don't like it. They certainly can't be up to anything good. What did you *really* do to piss them off, anyway?!"

"Ben, nothing. Seriously, absolutely nothing! Jet wouldn't date Crystal. I wouldn't date Jace after I learned more about him. Apparently, they're both just batshit crazy and have deep-seated rejection issues! They probably belong together, honestly."

Ben scoffed, rising from his seat. "Well, it's time to see to what we owe the honor of this second visit of the evening, I suppose..."

"Wait for Jet," Morgan suggested. "The set is done. He'll be out in a few minutes." Ben nodded, sinking back onto his bar stool but keeping his eyes on the couple at the bar—something Jet had also been doing. "How'd she get in here, anyway?"

Morgan wasn't sure how Crystal had entered *Dirty Martini* in the first place. They were usually pretty strict about carding at the door. Then again, Crystal had proven rather adept at sneaking into and out of *Cold Brew* earlier, so maybe she managed to evade the bouncer entirely.

"What are you going to say to them?" Morgan asked, peering quizzically at Ben.

"I haven't decided yet, but they've had more than enough chances to keep their distance. I'm willing to bet they didn't realize I'd be here. They may not have realized *you'd* be here. This may have been a brother-to-brother visit that we accidentally intruded on."

"Oops," Morgan said, grinning.

"Big oops," Ben replied.

JET

He noticed them enter through the front door. From what he'd seen, Crystal had someone distract the bouncer long enough to slink in, covered from behind by Jace's broad body. It was nearly impossible to continue through the end of the song, knowing they were sitting at the bar, probably looking for him. It's not that he was afraid of Jace for himself, but he certainly wasn't okay with him harassing Morgan.

As soon as the set ended, Jet dropped his guitar in the back room. Without stopping to talk to Morgan and Ben, he walked in the direction of the bar area. He hoped they wouldn't follow, as he didn't want them any more involved in this than they already were—but he knew they would. As he came up on Crystal and Jace throwing a shot back in unison, he glared at them.

"What the hell are you doing here?" Jet growled through gritted teeth, trying to retain his composure.

"Ahh, Jethro! Good show, bro. Good to see you, too. We didn't really get a chance to talk earlier, you know? Rude interruptions and all." Jace said, his words oozing with fakeness. Jet rolled his eyes just as Ben appeared by his side. "Oh, you again? I didn't realize you traveled in a pack now."

"Yeah, we take care of our own around here, unlike in your world, it seems." Ben glared at Jace. "I thought I told you to stay away from my staff. Twice."

"It's a public place. My girlfriend and I just wanted to have a few drinks is all. Who would have thought we'd wind up in the same bar my dearest brother was performing at." Jace smirked.

"Your *girlfriend* isn't even old enough to be here," Ben pointed out.

"Semantics," Jace muttered. "She's plenty old enough in the ways that matter... if you know what I mean." He winked suggestively at Jet and Ben. The blatant disrespect was more than either could handle. Simultaneously, Ben pulled his arm back and threw one rapid-fire punch square into Jace's nose while Jet pulled his leg back and kicked him in the groin with perfect precision.

Morgan's jaw dropped as the crowd separated, and Jace fell into a heap on the barroom floor, groaning. A cheer circulated the bar as he hit the ground. *I guess he didn't make many friends in his brief time here,* Jet thought. *Not surprising. He's a dick.* Blood poured from Jace's nose, but he didn't even try to stop it. His hands were otherwise occupied with gripping his crotch in agony. Crystal dove toward Jace, throwing herself at him in an array of dramatics worthy of an Academy Award.

"Baby, are you okay? How could they do this to you?"

Crystal's sobs were returned only with a scowl. "Get off me, you dumb bitch!" he roared.

Tears formed in Crystal's eyes, and her lower lip shuddered. "What?" she whispered.

"You heard me! Get off. I'm finished with you. You're nothing but a stupid kid."

"... but I thought—" Crystal's voice trailed off.

"Thought what?" Jace growled. "That I would be your happily ever after?" He laughed in her face. "You were nothing but a pawn in a game you're too young and stupid to know anything about. Now, back the fuck up off me, slut. Go back to school. You've got a lot to learn."

Crystal rose from her perch beside Jace and buried her face in her hands. She glanced over at Ben and Morgan, then down at Jace again. "I'm sorry," she muttered in the direction of Morgan, Ben, and Jet, then bolted for the door, failing to contain the sobs that escaped as she ran from the bar.

"Follow her," Ben said to Morgan. "Make sure she's okay. Jet and I have this handled." He glanced down at Jace again. Someone had given him a pile of napkins to hold against his bleeding nose, and he seemed as if he was in somewhat less acute pain. Heaven knew he'd be sore for a while, though.

Morgan nodded and followed Crystal out the door.

"Ben," Jet started, his voice low.

"Yeah?"

"I appreciate all you've done for me, but I quit."

Complicated

JET

Chapter 30

"Quit?" Ben asked. "You can't quit. You just started!"

"Yeah, I know. And *Cold Brew* is great. But I feel like since I started, Morgan's had nothing but problems. *You've* had nothing but problems, too."

Jet looked Ben in the eye, then gestured to Jace, who was still on the ground but had moved to a sitting position. He was leaning against the bottom of the bar, and someone nearby looked to be offering cursory medical attention in the form of a wadded-up handful of paper towels and a glass of water.

"I don't want anyone to have to deal with this bullshit because of me and my—my family. It isn't fair. I didn't mean for any of this to happen... I just wanted a job."

"Listen, Jet... We don't always get what we want. Sometimes, we do eventually, but life has a funny way of getting us there. Don't abandon the path set out before you over a few bumps in the road. I can handle a few unexpected surprises —it's what's gotten me this far. You don't go traipsing through jungles around the world without experiencing a few hiccups along the way. It doesn't mean you abandon all you've worked for, though. The very existence of *Cold Brew* and *Charmed to Table* as they exist today, not to mention Gia and me, is a real-life story of things not going the way I'd wanted—but coming full circle to become a dream come true."

Jet rolled his eyes at Ben. "You're being cheesy."

"It may be cheesy, but it's the truth. Morgan has had her fair share of bumps along the way. She's grown stronger for it. You've probably noticed that I look out for her the way I would for a daughter of my own. If I didn't think you working at *Cold Brew* was a good idea, you wouldn't be there. You wouldn't be standing here trying to quit—I'd be asking you to leave."

"I guess so."

"Maybe this isn't the best time or place to have this conversation. Let's get out of here. Grab your stuff while I talk to our friend Jace about his... options. Then, we'll check on Crystal, drop Morgan off at home, and talk this through."

Jet nodded, gave his brother a prod with his foot, and mumbled, "You got what you deserved," as he walked toward the back room to collect his guitar and other belongings.

MORGAN

Morgan followed closely behind Crystal as she ran away from *Dirty Martini.* "Crystal, stop! Wait up!" Morgan called, feeling the few drinks she'd had over the course of the night a bit more as she jogged to catch up.

Crystal glanced behind her, slowed, then finally stopped. She shrugged. "It's not like I have any place to go anyway," she mumbled. "That dickhead drove me here, and I don't even have bus fare to get home."

"Crystal, Jace is an asshole. I tried to warn you. I'm sorry for what he put you through, but listen; I've known you for a while, and this isn't you. You're better than this—and you're better than him. Find someone your own age. Someone who respects you. The person you find yourself smiling around without even realizing it. Someone who makes you laugh but who you also feel comfortable telling your deepest secrets, knowing they won't judge you."

As Morgan spoke, she couldn't help but realize that Jet was quickly becoming all those things to her. She shook her head back and forth quickly, trying to push the realization from her mind. Crystal wiped a tear from her face, giving Morgan an apologetic look.

"I'm sorry we gave you and Jet such a hard time, Morgan. It wasn't my idea to follow or threaten you—except for that night at *Charmed to Table* with my friends—but I was just there trying to run into Jet. I didn't even know you guys were even a thing until I saw you together there."

"We weren't. We aren't. It's complicated."

"You sure look like you are when you're together—and if you're really not, then maybe you should be."

Morgan chuckled. "We'll see. I don't even want to think about that right now. Anyway, let's go back to the bar to meet up with Ben and Jet. I'm sure Ben will be happy to drive you home. He's already gotta take Jet and me, but... uh... actually, it's going to be an *incredibly* tight squeeze. I could take the bus, and you can ride with them."

"Thanks. I appreciate it. Maybe just a taxi?"

"That probably makes more sense. Come on." Morgan turned and reached for Crystal's hand, leading her back in the direction of *Dirty Martini*. On the front steps, she saw Ben and Jet craning their necks first in one direction, then the other, clearly looking for the two women. As Jet's eyes connected with Morgan's, she gave him a quick wave. He nudged Ben in the ribs with his elbow, and the men began walking toward them.

"Everything okay?" Ben asked, meeting Crystal's eyes, then shifting his gaze to Morgan.

"Yes. I'm sorry, Ben. Sorry, Jet. I didn't mean to cause so much trouble. Would it be okay if—well—would you mind calling me a taxi? I can pay you back later this week at *Cold Brew*."

"Of course. My treat. We will wait for you to get into the car safely." Ben paused, seemingly deep in thought. "Does Jace, by any chance, know where you live?" Ben asked, rubbing his chin. He seemed concerned.

"No. We've only been to his place together. I still live with my parents. They'd murder me if they knew I'd dated him—or anyone his age, for that matter."

Ben pulled out his phone, looked up the number of the most reputable taxi service in the area and called. As they waited for the vehicle to arrive, they all sat on the rock wall bordering the front of the bar, kicking their feet against the stones.

The silence was palpable. No one knew what to say. On the one hand, Morgan wanted to throw herself into Jet and fall against his chest, seeking the comfort she'd felt earlier. On the other, they hadn't even had their "date" after all the chaos of the evening and the way things fell into place. *Was dating off the table entirely after this fiasco?*

Once again, Morgan had no idea what they were, weren't,

or could be. *If this is meant to be, isn't it supposed to be easy?* Morgan thought to herself. *This is anything but easy.*

Decisions Made

JET

WHEN ALL WAS SAID and done, Crystal took a cab home, and the men dropped Morgan off at her apartment. "We have to wait a minute," Ben said.

"Why?" Jet asked.

Ben pointed up to Morgan's window. In a few moments, enough time for her to make it up the stairs and into her apartment, her lights flipped on, then off, then on again. This was a habit she'd gotten into whenever Ben or Gia drove her home. It let him know she made it in safely.

"Now we can go," Ben said, chuckling.

"It's good that you look out for her the way you do," Jet said.

"I told you—*Cold Brew* is like family! We look out for our own."

Jet nodded. "I know she appreciates it. So do I."

During the remainder of the drive back to Jet's car, he and Ben discussed Jet's employment at *Cold Brew*.

"I just don't want to stay there if it creates unnecessary drama for anyone. In the brief period I've been there, it's only led to trouble for you and Morgan. Think about it."

"None of which was actually your *fault*," Ben pointed out. "You can't fix other peoples' crazy. Anyway, it's not like we didn't need a little bit of excitement around here. For a minute there, I kind of felt like a superhero swooping in out there by the dumpsters to save the day," Ben said, releasing the steering wheel with one hand to pose in a bicep curl to indicate his strength.

Jet chuckled. "Okay, okay, Superman. I just don't want to make things harder for Morgan. It's already confusing. You weren't wrong when you said she and I were doing *something*. Only, I don't know *what* we're doing. I wasn't looking for anything. I didn't want anything—I just wanted a job. Now, all that I do know is that it doesn't seem to be getting any simpler. It may be better for all of us if I just... disappear."

"Like you did from your last town?"

"How'd you know? Did Morgan—"

"Morgan didn't say anything. It's just blatantly obvious that you're running from something. I can tell because I was just like you." Ben glanced away from the road as they waited at a stoplight, eyeing Jet. "Why do you think I spent over the last decade jumping from one foreign country to another? From one isolated rainforest locale to the next? I got scared and ran away. It took me a long time to figure out that what I really needed was back here. It was my life with Gia. No amount of success or adventure could have filled that hole— and believe me, I tried. I'm *incredibly* fortunate for the way things worked out in the end. Don't make the same mistake. You might not get so lucky!"

"Maybe just a break?" Jet asked. "To let things settle down?"

"From the café or Morgan?"

"Maybe both..." Jet ran his hand through his hair, brushing it off the sides of his face. "Just to figure things out."

"Listen, Jet, I'm no expert, but I think running away from this—even for a 'break,' as you call it—is a bad idea, but I'll leave it up to you. My break took many years to return from." Glancing behind to be sure no one was behind them, Ben paused the vehicle at a stop sign for an extended pause. He placed a hand on Jet's shoulder firmly and looked him in the eye.

"I'll be roasting beans tomorrow morning at *Cold Brew* either way. If you show up, we'll forget this conversation ever happened. If you aren't there, if and when you're ready, we can discuss the terms of returning. I can't make any promises about holding your position, though. I can't leave Morgan alone again to juggle so many hours—and she deserves to remain a manager. At first, working all her waking moments was a good distraction, but now it's too much. She has other goals, other dreams."

Jet nodded, understanding Ben's terms and knowing that tomorrow was make or break.

When they arrived at *Cold Brew* to drop Jet off at his car, which he left parked directly in front of Ben's camera should someone—a certain twin brother, perhaps—feel the need to do harm, Jet glanced at Ben as he stepped out of the car.

"Mind if I stop in to use the restroom before heading home?" Jet asked, avoiding Ben's gaze by staring directly at the café instead.

"Sure thing. Just do me a favor and lock up when you're all done in there. I've gotta get home for some shuteye. Early morning roasting the beans and all!"

Jet nodded, breathing a sigh of relief that Ben wouldn't be

waiting for him—let alone accompanying him inside. He wondered, for a moment, if Ben was already onto his plan... He shrugged. *No matter,* he thought. *It is what it is.*

He tossed his guitar case into his car, waving Ben off. As soon as he'd driven away, Ben pulled the guitar from its case and propped it against his passenger seat, leaving the case empty.

Jet walked into *Cold Brew* through the back door, his guitar case slung over his shoulder, much lighter than usual. He headed to the back area of the café, grabbed the few items he had stored in his cubby, leaving the space empty, and tossed them in his guitar case. *Might as well make things easy on Ben. He'll know not to expect me as soon as he comes back here to get the raw coffee beans.*

As he turned to leave the room, his eyes caught Morgan's storage cubby. Inside, he noticed the clothes she'd been wearing at work earlier, several hair ties and clips, a brush, a stick of deodorant, some miscellaneous makeup items, and a bottle of perfume. Without even thinking, he picked up the bottle and spritzed some into the air, immediately filling the small space with her scent.

Jet took a deep breath through his nose, and, for a moment, tears threatened. He knew that if he walked away now, things would probably never be the same for them—and he may very well lose any possibility of being with her, even as friends. He gulped hard, grabbed a hair tie, sprayed it with another spray of perfume, and tucked it into his pants pocket.

He walked to the front, pulled a bag of the same Brazilian blend coffee he'd shared with Morgan off the retail rack, leaving the space intentionally unfilled with another from behind and tucked it into his guitar case. *Ben will understand.*

Finally, Jet threw a twenty-dollar bill on the counter for the coffee, then walked out of the room and left the building, locking the door behind him. He knew he was running away again, but he couldn't help it.

The thought of Morgan terrified him, mainly because he wanted her so much.

It was just too much.

Hasty Conclusions

MORGAN

WHEN MORGAN ARRIVED at *Cold Brew* the next morning, she was in decent spirits. The commute had gone smoothly, and the events of the night before were somewhat duller in her mind. *What's with the drama lately, though?* She rolled her eyes as she walked into the café and found Ben sitting on the stool in front of the massive machine roasting beans. *What's he doing here?*

Ben wore a somber expression as he dumped a massive bag of coffee beans into the roaster's loader. When he noticed her, he looked up and plastered an obviously fake smile across his face.

"What's wrong?" Morgan asked. "You don't usually roast today." Morgan's eyes scanned the room. She knew she was a few minutes late but had figured Jet would hold down the fort and get things started without her. At this point, he knew how to open the store on his own.

"Where's Jet?" she asked.

Ben glanced up from the roaster again, now trying to keep his expression emotionless. "Jet is..." Ben's voice trailed off as he tried to determine the best way to explain their conversation the night before, then arriving at the coffee shop only to find Ben's cubby empty. "He's—"

"He quit," Morgan interrupted. "Things got a tiny bit too complicated, and he ran away, didn't he?" Ben was silent. "Didn't he?" she repeated.

Ben, still having no words for the situation, simply shrugged and nodded. Morgan scoffed and stormed back toward the door she'd just come in through. "Can you cover for me for an hour? I'll be back before the worst of the morning rush, I promise."

"What are you—"

"I'm getting Jet back here. He's being an ass. And he forgets that I know where he lives."

Ben seemed to know better than to argue with Morgan about the topic at hand, so he waved her out the door and began opening the café on his own. The beans could wait.

"Jet!" Morgan started shouting his name before she even reached the top of the stairs. When she arrived at his door, she pounded on it until Jet opened it wide enough to poke his head out. When he saw Morgan, he stepped outside into the hallway, leaving it open only a crack.

"Morgan—what are you doing here?"

Morgan tried to ignore the fact that he was wearing only

boxers, and his dark, speckled eyes were wide with surprise, framed perfectly by his tussled, bedhead hair. "No... what are *you* doing here? You're supposed to be at work. What the fuck, Jet?"

"Morgan, listen. Now isn't a great time. Can we talk about this later?"

"No. We can talk about it here. Now." As Morgan spoke, a light in Jet's apartment flickered on. "Wait, is someone else here?"

Jet glanced behind him, noticing his bedroom light had been turned on. As Morgan peered past him, her jaw fell. She caught the silhouette of a woman walking from Jet's bed toward the kitchen, wearing only a long tee shirt. Her eyes widened in shock as the realization hit...

"Crystal!?" Morgan couldn't say anymore before the tears came. She wasn't even sure why she was crying. It's not like she and Jet were together. Not really, anyway. They weren't a couple. Jet was free to do whatever he wanted—but Crystal!?

"No, no. Morgan, it isn't like that," Jet tried to explain, quickly realizing the conclusion she'd drawn, but it was too late. Morgan turned and raced down the steps, out the door, and toward the bus stop. By the time Jet had his shoes on and made it to the street, she'd already hopped on the first bus to pull up.

Jet

Jet walked slowly back to his apartment, feeling defeated. He knew exactly what it looked like to Morgan, but nothing had happened between him and Crystal. Their interactions were entirely innocent. She needed a safe place to stay for the night after Jace made several threats, and he couldn't turn her away after what his brother had already done to the poor girl.

When Jet arrived back at his apartment, Crystal was standing in the kitchen pouring two cups of coffee from the now-cold brew they'd made when she'd come to his place the night before.

"Is she okay?" Crystal asked as she put one of the cups in the microwave. "I'm sorry. I didn't even know she was at the door. I had just woken up. I guess I wasn't thinking."

"It wasn't your fault. I didn't get to talk to her," Jet said, running his fingers through his hair to brush it off his face. "She was already gone."

"Maybe if I talk to her? Explain what happened and that it really isn't what it looks like. I can only imagine what she thinks... I'm sorry, Jet. I didn't mean to cause more problems between you two. Especially after what we talked about last night. You two clearly belong with each other."

"Maybe we can do it together. She's probably on her way back to *Cold Brew* right now."

"Get dressed, then," Crystal directed. "We'll fix it. You helped me last night, now it's my turn. My parents are already going to kill me for staying out all night—what's another couple of hours?" Crystal grabbed the clothes she'd worn the night before from the top of the dresser and walked toward the bathroom to change.

From the bathroom, she called out, "Thanks for letting me have the bed last night. I hope the couch wasn't too uncomfortable."

"It was fine," Jet said as he grabbed his own clothes from his drawers. As Crystal got ready in the bathroom, Jet did the same in record time. His heart was pounding as he imagined what Morgan must be thinking. Of course, all of this had to happen right after he'd come to the conclusion that he wanted to be with her—entirely with her. Only with her.

Ironically, his talk with Crystal the night before had led him to realize that he was falling in love with Morgan, and now it threatened the possibility of achieving that future. He didn't realize how sad he must look, but as Crystal emerged, she looked concerned.

"Don't worry, Jet. We'll fix it. Come on. Let's go. First stop, *Cold Brew.*"

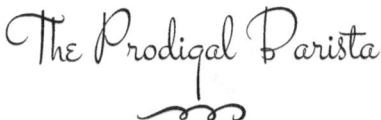

The Prodigal Barista

MORGAN

Chapter 33

MORGAN SWEPT into *Cold Brew* and, without a word to Ben or anyone else, headed to the back room to freshen up. Her tears had subsided during the bus ride from Jet's apartment to the café, but she still needed a few minutes to compose herself before facing Ben and the customers.

As she glanced at Jet's empty cubby, the tears threatened to return, but she successfully fought them back. *No. I won't cry again. He wasn't mine to cry over.* As her hair fell into her eyes, Morgan searched for the spare hair tie she always kept in her cubby. *What the hell? I know I put it here. Maybe Gia borrowed it?*

She rolled her eyes, then swept her hair behind her ears and held it back with two clips instead. Finally, Morgan splashed some cold water on her face from a bottle she

191

found in the supply area. *Whatever. It's fine. Everything is fine.* Just as she was about to emerge and make her way to the front of the store, Ben cornered her, standing at the door.

"What happened?" Ben asked.

"I don't want to talk about it. Can we just work?"

"Does it involve Crystal?"

"Why are you asking? How did you know? Did you know they were getting together?"

"Not exactly. I ask because she and Jet are out front asking for you..."

Morgan groaned. "Tell them I'm not here," Morgan said, putting her hands over her face.

"You know just as well as they do that you're *always* here," Ben pointed out.

"Well, then tell them I *was* here, but now I'm gone. I went home sick. Or I didn't come back after I left Jet's apartment. In fact, I do feel sick. I think I need to go home. Right now. Out the back door."

"Morgan, I still don't know what happened—but I can venture a guess—and I think you need to talk to them. Things aren't always what they seem, you know."

"Sometimes they are, though. Sometimes things are *exactly* what they seem." As Morgan finished her sentence, Jet's face appeared, peering around the corner at her. He looked sad, almost broken.

"Too late to escape now," Ben told her. "That ship has sailed. Talk to them. I've got the front."

Morgan glared at Ben as he walked away. Jet took his place in the doorway, Crystal following closely behind.

"We need to talk to you," Jet began. "None of this is what it looks like. I promise." He gestured to Crystal before reaching into his pocket, slowly pulling up and holding Morgan's hair tie out to her.

She snatched it away, the faint scent of her perfume tickling her nose. "Why did you...?"

"Because... If I wasn't coming back—and I wasn't planning on it at the time—I needed to bring a piece of you with me."

"Then, why are you back?" Morgan asked.

"Because I realized something last night," Jet said.

"While you were with *her?*" She motioned toward Crystal.

"Actually, yes—but not in the way that you think. We talked about you. Literally, the entire time, we talked about you. Crystal needed a place to stay where Jace wouldn't find her after he learned where she lived and threatened her. We talked as friends. She slept on the bed. I stayed on the couch. Now, the situation with Jace is in the hands of the police. Crystal spoke with them on our way here. Nothing happened between us, and I realized something..."

"It doesn't matter, anyway. It's not my place to care. It's never been my place."

"But, Morgan, that's the thing. You *do* care. And I do, too. The truth of the matter is that I care more about you than I have for anyone in a long time, and I'm not willing to let that go. Whether I work here or not, it's rare—and I don't think we should let it go."

Morgan sniffed as she glanced at Jet, then Crystal. "Nothing happened? Nothing at all?" she asked, her voice quivering slightly. She knew she had no claim on Jet, but it still hurt to think of the two of them together.

"Nothing," Crystal confirmed. "And I'm sorry, again, for all the trouble I caused. I've been having a tough time lately, but I think Jet set me straight. He's a great friend, and I know he is miserable at the thought of not seeing you every day at *Cold Brew.*" She reached out and squeezed Jet's shoulder.

"With that said," she continued, "I'm going to get going. Time to face the music from my parents for arriving home at...

whatever time it is! I'm sure I'll have to explain about Jace, too, since the police will expect to speak with me about it." Crystal rolled her eyes. "Not to mention that I'll probably be grounded for life, so if you don't ever see *me* back here, there's your explanation."

Jet smiled at Crystal. "Call if Jace tries anything else. Ben and I both have your back."

"So do I," Morgan chimed in. "And I'm sorry for jumping to conclusions. Now I'm only mad at Jet for thinking he could get out of his employment at *Cold Brew* so easily. Am I really *that* awful of a manager?" A slight grin crept up the corners of Morgan's lips.

"The worst," Jet said, grinning. "But, can I have my job back anyway?"

Crystal chuckled before giving a quick wave and heading toward the front. "Hope you two can work it out. You both seem happier since you met. Anyone with eyes can see that."

JET

"So?" Jet asked.

"So what?" Morgan responded.

"So... Can I have my job back?"

"I'd imagine that'd be up to Ben since he hired you, no?"

Jet chuckled. "I already asked him. He told me it was out of his hands and that I should ask my manager." He pretended to scoff. "I informed him that she's a bit of a hard-ass, but he refused to hire me back without her consent. The nerve!"

"A hard-ass, huh?" Morgan asked.

"That's what I said."

Morgan smirked as she pulled out her phone and brought

up the video of Jet wiggling his ass as he did his cleaning dance behind the counter.

"Would a hard-ass manager let her employees get away with *this?*" She held up her phone for Jet to see. "Maybe you just need to open your eyes to my extraordinary managerial prowess and accept how lucky you really are!" she said, grinning.

"Managerial prowess, huh?"

"Absolutely. I'm a bit of an expert at being cool, calm, and collected. You know. Getting shit done and whatnot... and I don't usually let employees return after they quit suddenly, without giving me any notice."

As Morgan spoke, Jet pulled up a photo on his phone and held it out to her.

"Cool, calm, and collected, you say?" he asked.

"Okay, there may be an occasional exception," Morgan admitted, hiding her face after glancing at the photo of her sprawled out on the floor of the back room, surrounded by toilet paper rolls.

"Well, if we're making exceptions, can we make one more?"

"And what would that be?"

"My super understanding, perfectly together, extraordinarily competent—and not to mention stunningly beautiful —manager: May I please return to *Cold Brew* under your expert managerial supervision?"

"I think that can be arranged," Morgan said, smiling at Jet.

Jet beamed and placed his hand under Morgan's chin, pulling her in towards him until his lips were pressed against his.

"Thank you," he murmured into her lips.

"Anytime," she said, pulling away from him. "Hey, Jet... You officially restart your employment with *Cold Brew* as of tomorrow morning and—" She let out a few loud fake coughs. "Hey, Ben?" she called out.

"Yep? Everything okay back there?" Ben's voice rang out from the front of the store.

"Do you mind covering one more shift? I... I think I need a sick day. I promise our new, old employee and I will cover every single shift next week." Morgan paused for a moment, glancing at Jet.

"I think I need a nap," she added, winking at Jet.

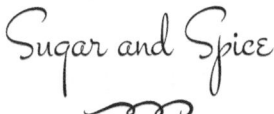

Sugar and Spice

JET

Chapter 34

MORGAN AND JET climbed the steps to his apartment at record speed. When they reached the top, Jet pulled the door open.

"Ladies first," he said, gesturing for Morgan to enter.

"Why, thank you," she said, grinning. "Very gentlemanly of you."

"You know... I'm not *always* a gentleman..." he trailed off.

"Is that so?"

"It is."

"What sort of ungentlemanly things do you do?" Morgan asked, raising an eyebrow, a flirtatious smile forming on her lips.

"Come here. I'll show you." Jet pulled Morgan close and

pressed his lips against hers, pushing her firmly but gently backward until the door closed behind them. Now inside, with Morgan's back resting against the door, Jet bit her lower lip gently, then moved to kiss her ear, traveling downward with little kisses and the occasional nibble until he reached the middle of her neck.

Morgan moaned. "Still... pretty... gentlemanly," she managed to mutter in between breaths.

"Oh really?" Jet asked, pulling away to stare Morgan directly in the eyes. "And is that what you want? A non-gentleman?" Jet's voice was husky, filled with desire. Morgan nodded shyly. "Tell me what you want, then, Morgan."

Morgan pressed harder against Jet's body, trying to use body language to indicate exactly what she wanted. "No, Morgan. *Tell* me what you want. I want to hear it."

"I want you," she breathed.

"What do you want from me?"

"Everything. I want to feel you."

"Want to feel me where, good girl?"

Morgan groaned. "Everywhere."

Jet reached under Morgan and lifted her in his arms the same way he had the first time they'd napped together. He carried her to his bed, kissing her quickly between each step until he reached the bed and placed her down. With his knees on either side of her legs, Jet leaned over her to rest his body over hers.

"Everywhere?" he asked. Morgan nodded. "Say it again. Tell me."

"I want to feel you everywhere. I want you inside me."

This time, it was Jet's turn to groan. "Anything you want, Princess. Ask, and you shall receive."

He kissed Morgan's forehead, moved down to her mouth, then made his way to her neck and chest. Placing a hand behind her back, he sat her up in the bed and supported her from behind as he pulled her shirt over her head, then unclasped her bra and tossed it aside. Jet's hands wandered across Morgan's stomach, tracing teasing lines over her breasts, circling her nipple area, then moving down to her waist and following the elastic over her stomach—just above where her pants rested on her hips.

His caresses were gentle, playing across Morgan's body, exploring—and causing her to rise upward, pushing her skin against his fingertips, begging for more of his touch.

"What's wrong, Morgan?" Jet asked in response to Morgan's silent pleas for more attention.

"You're teasing me," she responded, pouting.

"And?"

Morgan's hands wandered down and over the front of Jet's pants, one hand cupping him over the fabric, feeling his hardness, the other tugging on his waistband. "Give me," she said simply.

"All you had to do was ask," Jet said. Climbing off Morgan and standing beside the bed, Jet removed his clothing, dropping it at his feet. "One problem," he started.

"What's that?" she asked, eyeing him curiously.

"Uneven distribution," he said, gesturing to her pants, which he'd begun to pull downward, over her ankles and off. "Now, *that's* real beauty." He gazed longingly at Morgan, taking in the image of her lying on his bed in only her lacy black panties. He committed the vision to memory as best he could—her stomach, soft and welcoming; her breasts, perfectly rounded and sized; and the way her hair fell over her shoulders, framing her face. Morgan's breathtaking green eyes peered up at Jet, her breathing heavy with wanting.

"Just one more thing to achieve true perfection..." Jet said. Morgan blushed as he bent a finger around the elastic of her panties and tugged them down and off. "*Now,* you're perfect," he said, pressing his mouth to her belly button in a quick kiss, then moving his lips down over the smooth skin of her abdomen and tracing the strip of hair on her mound with his tongue. Rather abruptly, Jet placed a hand on each of Morgan's thighs and pushed them apart, teasing the outside of her lips with a gentle blow, then circling her clit with his thumb, intentionally avoiding her most sensitive part with his barely-there touch. Gia arched her back slightly, causing her body to rise to meet his fingers, begging for more.

"Jettt," Morgan whined.

"Yes, good girl?"

"You're driving me crazy... More," she pleaded.

Jet chuckled. "In that case, I like you when you're crazy." He spread her lips and licked the length of her pussy, sending a shiver through Morgan. She groaned as he formed his mouth around her clit, sucking, then sweeping his tongue across it several times. Then, he placed a finger inside her, curled it, and began pumping it slowly in and out of Morgan. "Is this what you wanted, pretty girl? You're so wet for me. How long have you wanted this?"

"Since the moment I met you," Morgan admitted. "Even when I didn't think I liked you." As Jet sped up, the sensations from his finger and mouth working on her together were more than Morgan could take. She closed her eyes and tilted her head back as an orgasm rushed over her.

Dazed and breathless, after several moments, she opened her eyes to find herself face-to-face with Jet. "Oh my God, Jet," Morgan said. "That was incredible."

"Oh, did you think I was done?" Jet asked, grabbing the back of Morgan's head as he placed his lips against hers and kissed her deeply, separating her lips with his tongue. Then, he pulled away. "Not even close," he murmured as he reached into the drawer beside the nightstand and pulled out a condom.

"I need to be inside you," Jet said, unrolling the condom over his length. "Now. Right now. Are you okay with that, Beauty?" Morgan groaned, the combination of her arousal and his pet names taking away any possibility of rational thought.

"Mmhmm," she mumbled. She wouldn't have been able to say no at that point, even if she'd wanted to—which she hadn't.

"Tell me."

"I want you inside me."

"How bad?"

"So bad. Please, Jet. I need you to fill me."

Jet rolled his head back and groaned as he slid into her. They moved together gently, hips rolling into each other, pushing Jet in as deep as possible. When Jet couldn't stand it anymore, he sped up, grinding into Morgan as she scratched a trail down his back and grabbed his ass.

"Baby, turn over," Jet asked, giving her room to get onto her knees. As she did so without a word, he moved behind her, entering her pussy from behind and gripping her hair as he pumped into her. Both wild with lust and pent-up desire, their animalistic needs came before anything else. Morgan's body began to tense up as another orgasm built.

"Jet... I'm—" Morgan didn't get to finish her sentence before the wave crashed over her, sending her into a moan.

"Did you—"

"Yeah," Morgan said, breathing heavily.

Jet groaned. The knowledge that he'd sent her over the edge again triggered his own climax.

"Fuck," he shouted as he pumped a few final times into her, then collapsed, still inside. For a few moments, he remained there, holding himself up slightly with his forearms to avoid resting the entire weight of his body on Morgan. When he went to move off her, she reached around him and pulled him back.

"No. Stay for a couple more minutes. Just like this."

"Anything you say, Princess," Jet said as he settled back into position over Morgan.

Falling

MORGAN

Chapter 35

As soon as Morgan's eyes fluttered open, she realized that at some point after she fell asleep, Jet had moved to lie on his side next to her. He had one arm set beneath the pillow on which her head rested, and the other was placed gently over her hip. Morgan's gaze fell on Jet's face, which wore an expression that could only be described as peaceful. She wondered whether this was how he always looked when he slept or if it was because of their earlier... activities.

Morgan, stop watching him sleep. You're being creepy, she told herself as she tried to stealthily slip out of the bed without waking him. After a few attempts via different maneuvers, she managed to get out of Jet's bed, throw her clothes on, and make her way into the kitchen.

She needed water. As she walked to the sink and turned

the water on, though, the empty coffee pot caught her eye. *My turn*, she thought as she grabbed the new, unopened bag of Brazilian brew Jet had left out on the counter. She made light work of preparing a pot of coffee, hoping the wafting aroma would bring Jet to the kitchen as it had with her the last time she awoke in his apartment.

Sure enough, as the coffee began percolating, Morgan heard a yawn and a long groan that likely accompanied a stretch, followed by movement from the bedroom. Suddenly, she felt nervous! *Now? NOW I get nervous?! After everything last night?*

She leaned against the counter, holding a container filled with sugar packets, trying to appear nonchalant. Then, fretting that it looked too forced, she rushed to try a different stance before he entered the kitchen. Somehow, in the rapid motion, she lost her balance. Her feet became tangled in each other—and down she went into a pile on the floor just in time for Jet to enter the room.

"You sure seem to spend a lot of time sitting around on the floor, surrounded by messes," Jet observed, a smile creeping up his face.

"I... I fell," Morgan stated the obvious.

"I noticed," Jet said, putting his hand out for her. "Did you ever consider that employment in the hot beverage field might not be the best option for someone who's clearly prone to klutziness?" He glanced over at the full coffee pot and mugs arranged on the counter.

"Awww, wifey, you made coffee," he joked, grinning. She couldn't help but return his smile, reaching up to grab his outstretched hand.

As Jet pulled Morgan to her feet, she gestured to the coffee. "I did. I figured it was my turn. But, the only way you get to drink it is if you do me a favor first."

"The only way I get to drink it?!" Jet exclaimed. "It's *my* coffee!"

"Yeah, but I made it."

Jet narrowed his eyes at Morgan. "What's the favor?"

"I want you to teach me how to do those fancy latte designs you do!"

"You don't know how to make—"

"No! I told you—we don't do that at *Cold Brew*. Ben's more of a coffee purist. He really cares mostly about the brews. We have never done them before, anyway—but I was thinking about it, and it's really the perfect combination of my two passions: art and coffee. Therefore, you're the first to know that as Manager at *Cold Brew*, I hereby elect to implement a coffee art component to our beverages. We can even have a menu of designs! Now... teach, Master!"

Jet rubbed his chin thoughtfully. "Okay. I like it. And I can certainly do that, but... let's go back to *Cold Brew*. I need an espresso machine and some supplies."

Morgan nodded. "You got it! But first, coffee. Normal, ordinary, but always delicious, no-design coffee." She picked up the carafe and poured two mugs, handing one to Jet.

"Sounds like a plan," Jet agreed. "Thanks," he said, taking the beverage. Together, they sat on the couch, drinking the very same caffeinated beverages that had brought them together in the first place. Jet moved his hand to rest on Morgan's and gave it a gentle squeeze.

"Hey, Jet?" Morgan asked.

"Mmhmm?"

"At the risk of sounding needy, I feel like I have to ask... What are we?"

Jet looked pensive. "Hmm. I think it's safe to call you my girlfriend if you are okay with it." He turned to gaze deeply into her eyes. "I mean, I'd *like* you to be my girlfriend, anyway."

Morgan grinned as she wrapped her arms around Jet and brought one hand to his head, pushing his hair out of his eyes. "Yes, please." She pressed her lips to his and kissed him softly, then pulled away and rose to her feet. "And... I changed my mind."

"About what?" Jet asked, eyeing her curiously.

"You can teach me the craft of latte design at work tomorrow. It's not good to mix business with pleasure... and we're off work today. Let's keep focusing on the latter." Morgan winked at Jet, a flirtatious smile pulling her lips upward.

Jet's eyebrows rose, and his eyes widened, intrigued. "I mean, we are co-workers. You're my boss. And now my girlfriend, too. Isn't mixing business with pleasure kind of our... thing?"

"Maybe. But not today! Today, I'm not your manager. I'm only your girlfriend. Your girlfriend who wants nothing more than to return to bed with her boyfriend and be lazy for the rest of the day, do absolutely nothing productive, and not think about work until tomorrow morning."

"I think that can be arranged, girlfriend," Jet said, rising to his feet, lifting Morgan off the floor and carrying her, again, to his bed, where he laid her down and sat beside her.

"Hey, Jet?" Morgan started.

"Yes, pretty girl?"

"If we wind up falling asleep again, don't get up without me. I want to wake up next to you this time."

"Anything for you. As long as you promise the same."

"I promise," she said as Jet climbed over her and kissed her forehead softly. He inched lower and kissed her, pulling away only for a moment—just long enough to mumble, "Hey, barista girl, I think I'm falling for you."

"I fell for you the day I met you."

About the Author

Regina Bergen lives with her three children and two rescue dogs in the beautiful Hudson Valley region of New York. She has a B.A. in Environmental Studies and Latin American Studies and a Master's in Public Administration (neither of which she is currently using).

Before writing and editing full-time, Regina worked as a fundraiser at a global environmental conservation organization and spent several years as a stay-at-home mom. She loves the outdoors, animals, cooking, coffee, and spending her free time with her kids and pets.

Social Media – Get in Touch!

Facebook, TikTok, Instagram, and Goodreads: ReginaBergenAuthor

www.ReginaBergen.com

WritingbyRegina@gmail.com